I0712976

The Passage of Time

Elizabeth Chappelle

HUMMINGBIRD
PUBLISHING LTD

Hummingbird Publishing Ltd

Paperback – 978-1-78520-173-8

Contents

Note of Thoughts

The Passage of Time is a story of legacy how love and art ripple forward through generations, transforming but never fading. It explores how music becomes a vessel for memory, how grief can give way to creation, and how the heart, no matter its age, never stops listening for its song.

Lyrical and cinematic in tone, the novel moves between eras the post-war glamour of 1940s New York, the vibrant artistry of the modern world, and the stillness of later life blending romance, reflection, and the transcendence of music.

It reminds us that some stories do not end they change hands.

That love, once set to music, plays forever.

Synopsis

The Story

Part One: The Past Rekindled

Eleanor Thorpe, now in her eighties, returns to the Waldorf Astoria with her granddaughter. When she hears Eleanor's Waltz being played late at night, she follows the sound downstairs... and finds Henry Dalton at the piano, aged but still playing the song that once defined their love. Their reunion is heart-stopping and bittersweet, a reminder that some bonds never fade, even when life conspires to separate them.

Through tears and laughter, they share their memories: stolen dances during a time when social and familial expectations kept them apart, letters never sent, and the music that kept their souls intertwined.

Annabell watches in awe as her grandmother rediscovers her first love and in doing so, rediscovers herself.

Part Two: Inheritance of the Heart

After Henry's passing, Eleanor and Annabell grow closer, sharing stories of the man who taught Eleanor that love can live forever in a melody. When Eleanor herself dies peacefully years later, she leaves Annabell a small jewellery box and inside it, folded beneath her pearls, Annabell discovers a hidden letter from Henry.

In it, he reveals that Eleanor's Waltz was never finished that a second waltz was meant to be written someday, when love found its way back through time.

Grieving but inspired, Annabell teams up with Elias Moreau, a passionate young composer and archivist who shares her reverence for Dalton's work. Together, they complete the piece — Eleanor's Waltz II: The Beginning. Their collaboration blossoms into something deeper: a love built not on chance, but on destiny's quiet orchestration.

Part Three: The Legacy of Love

Their new composition becomes a global phenomenon — music critics call it "a bridge between generations, a sound that remembers." As their fame grows, Annabell and Elias are invited to perform at the Waldorf Astoria, in the same ballroom where Eleanor and Henry's story began.

The performance is electric — a culmination of passion, history, and healing. As the audience rises in ovation, Annabell feels her grandmother's presence all around her, the scent of lilies and the faint shimmer of figures waltzing just beyond the edge of light.

In the years that follow, Annabell and Elias travel the world, teaching, composing, and learning that love's truest expression isn't fame or perfection it's the courage to keep creating. Their partnership deepens into something sacred, a union of soul and sound.

Part Four: The Symphony for Eleanor

Inspired by everything her family's journey taught her, Annabell writes The Symphony for Eleanor, a full orchestral work capturing the life her grandmother lived, the love she shared, and the music that never stopped playing. When it premieres, audiences describe it as "the sound of time forgiving itself."

In its final movement, Annabell adds her own voice a new melody dedicated to Elias, the man who helped her transform memory into creation. It is not a farewell, but a continuation a promise that love, once found, echoes through eternity.

Part Five: The Passage of Time

Years later, Annabell and Elias grow older together, their love mellowed but unwavering. They teach, travel, and eventually settle in Florence, where the rhythms of daily life become their quiet music. After Elias passes away, Annabell continues to compose not for recognition, but for remembrance.

In her final years, she writes one last piece: The Last Note a simple, graceful waltz that begins with Eleanor's melody and ends with her own. When she finishes, she feels her grandmother's and Elias's presence around her one last time, and she smiles, knowing she has completed the song that began before she was born.

When she passes peacefully at her piano, her sheet music bears a final inscription:

For those who come after, keep playing. Love never ends.

Years later, The Last Note is performed at the Waldorf Astoria, in the very same ballroom where it all began. As the chandeliers shimmer, some in the audience swear they can see faint figures dancing a waltz, soft and eternal and know that love has, indeed, outlived time.

Prologue

Two Years Later

The melody of Eleanor's Waltz had never stopped playing.

Annabell carried it with her not just as music, but as memory, as pulse, as promise. It lived in the corners of her apartment in London, where sunlight fell across the piano that now sat by her window. It lived in the faint scent of lilies she always kept nearby. It lived, most of all, in the way she approached life slower now, more deliberate, as though she had finally learned to listen to what time was trying to tell her.

After Eleanor and Henry passed, she'd spent weeks replaying every detail of that final chapter of their lives their reunion, their peace, their parting. It had changed her. She no longer chased love in the hurried, uncertain way she once had. Instead, she allowed herself to trust that some things were meant to arrive in their own time just as Henry had found his way back to Eleanor after seventy years.

In her grief, she found creation.

Annabell composed her own piece a gentle, haunting melody she titled "Legacy." It began with the same opening notes as Eleanor's Waltz, but then branched off into something new — lighter, modern, full of promise. Where Eleanor's Waltz spoke of lost love and reunion, Legacy spoke of continuation, of hope beyond heartbreak.

She performed it publicly only once at a charity concert in Hyde Park, under the open night sky. When she played, she felt them there: her grandmother and Henry, dancing somewhere unseen, smiling with pride.

And as the final notes drifted into the air, she whispered quietly to herself, "For you, Nana. For all of it."

Chapter 1

The Waldorf Astoria's grand lobby sprawled before them, a timeless realm that seemed untouched by the passing decades. Nana Eleanor sank into one of the overstuffed armchairs near the entrance, her elegant figure almost dwarfed by its sheer size. The subdued glow of antique chandeliers lit her delicate features, which held an air of mystery beneath her graceful composure. Her long, silver hair, coiled neatly into a bun, gleamed like a crown. Annabelle paused, allowing her Nana a moment of reflection before wandering toward the reception desk.

Annabelle's eyes roamed the lobby, drinking in the splendor she'd only imagined during Nana's nostalgic tales. Marble floors shimmered beneath her feet, and towering columns soared into a gilded ceiling etched with intricate designs. The air itself seemed steeped in history, carrying whispers of a bygone era when her Nana had once graced these very halls. Each breath Annabelle took was tinged with a faint hint of polish and age-old wood, mingling with the faintest scent of fresh lilies arranged meticulously in porcelain vases.

Though the grandeur of the space enveloped her, Annabelle's heart fluttered with unease. She sensed that Nana's enthusiasm to return wasn't purely nostalgic. There was a weight to her longing, as if this journey was driven by a desire to reconcile with something lost long ago. The idea tugged at Annabell, igniting her romantic imagination. She herself yearned for the kind of love stories that novels promised, yet life so far had offered nothing close.

She reached the reception desk, her thoughts far away until the soft rustle of movement in the queue snapped her back to the present. A smile from the receptionist brought a faint blush to her cheeks. "Good evening, madam. Welcome to the Waldorf Astoria. Are you checking in?"

"Yes," Annabelle managed, her voice unsteady as she placed their passports on the counter. Clearing her throat, she gestured to Nana's insistence on Suite 56, located on the second floor with a view overlooking the city. Though she hadn't asked why the specific room was so crucial, Annabelle sensed its significance. To her relief, the room was available.

The check-in process felt like an eternity as Annabelle found her gaze wandering again. The lobby exuded an old-world charm: the warm hues of mahogany furniture paired with crimson and deep brown accents, the soft hum of indistinct chatter, and the occasional clink of glassware echoing from the bar beyond. Small brass lamps atop delicate side tables cast pools of light onto worn upholstery, their soft glow accentuating the timeworn beauty of the surroundings.

Key in hand, Annabelle rejoined Nana, who remained in the chair with her hands folded neatly atop her walking stick. Her expression was serene, yet Annabelle noticed the distant look in her eyes. How elegant she still was, Annabelle mused. Nana carried herself with an ageless dignity, a reminder of the woman she must have been—spirited, adventurous, and undoubtedly captivating. Despite her advanced age, a spark of that youthful fire lingered, echoing in Annabelle herself. Their likeness, both in appearance and temperament, often left Annabelle in awe.

She knelt by Nana's side and gently touched her hand. "Are you all right, Nana?"

Eleanor's gaze softened, and a wistful smile touched her lips. "Yes, dear. Just remembering."

Annabelle returned the smile. "You were daydreaming again."

Nana chuckled softly, a sound tinged with both mirth and melancholy. With a slow, deliberate effort, she rose from the armchair, leaning on her walking stick for support. Together, they began their journey to the elevator. As they passed through the lobby, Nana suddenly halted, her head tilting slightly as if catching an invisible thread in the air.

Annabelle looked at her with concern. "Nana? What is it?"

Eleanor took a deep breath, her chest rising as she inhaled a fragrance that seemed to materialize from nowhere. Her eyes gleamed with recognition, and her lips parted in a wide smile. The years seemed to fall away as she stood there, transfixed. She turned slowly, her gaze locked on the center of the lobby as though drawn by a force stronger than memory.

"What are you looking at?" Annabelle pressed, following her Nana's line of sight.

Eleanor's voice was barely a whisper, yet it carried the weight of a lifetime. "Just an old friend, dear."

Annabelle furrowed her brow and scanned the room, searching for the figure who had so clearly captivated her grandmother. But there was no one. Only the scattered crowd of travelers and hotel staff moving about, oblivious to the moment that had so profoundly affected Nana. She turned back, confusion etched across her face. "Who?"

"He's gone now," Eleanor replied softly, her smile fading into an expression of quiet sorrow. She turned back toward the elevator, her movements deliberate but heavy with emotion.

Annabelle lingered for a moment, torn between following her Nana and seeking out the source of her sudden joy. As the elevator chimed and its doors opened, she hurried to join her. Yet, the curiosity gnawed at her.

What—or who—had stirred such emotion in Nana's heart?

Why did the look in her eyes feel like the echo of a love story yet to be told?

Chapter 2

The year etched itself vividly in Eleanor's mind: 1946. She had been just 16 years old, swept away by the enchantment of her very first visit to New York City. Even now, the memory lingered, as if time had folded in on itself. Sitting on the plush armchair of their suite, Eleanor gazed out the window at the shimmering skyline, her breath catching in her chest. New York majestic and sprawling, still radiated the same magic it had all those decades ago, but now it bore the weight of her bittersweet recollections.

Annabell perched on the corner of a nearby chaise lounge, watching her grandmother in silence. Nana's profile, silhouetted by the soft glow of the city lights, looked regal yet heartbreakingly distant. Annabell felt an ache in her chest, a mix of admiration and longing. She had always known her Nana was more than the stories she shared. There were chapters left untold, hidden within those faraway expressions that crossed her face when she thought no one was looking.

"Nana?" Annabell asked softly. "What are you thinking about?"

Eleanor didn't answer immediately. Her gaze remained fixed on the cityscape, and her fingers absently traced the intricate carvings on the armrest of her chair. When she finally spoke, her voice was quiet, laced with wistfulness. "I remember the first time I saw this view. It was like stepping into a dream. The world felt... infinite." She hesitated, her lips trembling ever so slightly. "I felt infinite."

Annabell leaned forward, her curiosity piqued. "What was it like? Back then, I mean."

Eleanor closed her eyes briefly, letting the past rise within her like the swell of a tide. "It was 1946," she began. "The war had just ended, and the world was alive with hope. I arrived in this city with Lizzy, my maid, and Aunt Agatha, whom your great-grandmother trusted far too much." A faint smile played on her lips at the memory of her stern yet well-meaning chaperone. "Aunt Agatha had a knack for stifling anything remotely fun, but she couldn't dull the magic of that first night."

She paused, her chest tightening with the weight of what came next. "The city seemed to glow from within. The streets were filled with music, the air electric with possibility. Every moment felt like a promise waiting to be fulfilled." Her voice softened, taking on a note of sorrow. "And then there was him."

Annabell's heart skipped a beat at the change in her Nana's tone. "Him?" she echoed, leaning forward eagerly.

Eleanor didn't answer, not directly. Instead, she rose from her chair, walking slowly to the window. Her reflection merged with the glittering lights beyond, a ghost of her younger self staring back at her. "He was everything I didn't know I was looking for," she murmured. "Charming, daring... and utterly impossible."

Annabell felt a strange mix of emotions. She was captivated by her grandmother's story, but a pang of jealousy stirred within her. Who was this man who had left such a mark on Nana's heart? And why had she never heard of him until now?

"Did you love him?" Annabell asked hesitantly, her voice barely above a whisper.

Eleanor turned to her, her eyes shimmering with unshed tears. "Oh, my darling, I loved him more than words could ever express. But some loves…" She trailed off, her voice breaking slightly. "Some loves are not meant to last."

The room fell silent save for the faint hum of the city below. Annabell felt a lump rise in her throat. She couldn't bear to see her Nana so vulnerable, so fragile. "What happened?" she ventured cautiously.

Eleanor didn't answer immediately. She turned back to the window, her hands resting on the glass as if trying to touch the past. Her mind drifted back to that summer evening when everything had changed.

The year 1946 unfurled itself in her memory like a tapestry, vibrant and unyielding. The night she met him was her second evening in the city. They were at the Waldorf Astoria's grand ballroom, the air thick with the scent of jasmine and the murmur of laughter.

She had worn a pale blue dress, one that Lizzy had insisted brought out the colour of her eyes. Aunt Agatha, of course, had deemed it "too modern," but Eleanor had convinced her with a well-placed compliment about its modest neckline.

The moment he entered the room, she felt the world shift. He had a presence that commanded attention—a confidence that was magnetic without being overbearing. His dark hair was neatly combed, and his suit was perfectly tailored, but it was his eyes that captured her. They held a spark of mischief, tempered by something deeper, something she recognized even then as a kindred longing.

He had approached her without hesitation, bowing slightly as he extended his hand. "Would you honour me with a dance, Miss...?"

"Eleanor," she had replied, her voice trembling despite her best efforts. "Eleanor Thourpe."

"Eleanor," he repeated, as if savouring the taste of her name. "I'm Henry."

Annabell watched as her Nana's expression softened, a small smile tugging at the corners of her lips. It was as though the memory had brought her some measure of peace, even as it stirred her pain.

"Did you ever see him again?" Annabell asked, her voice thick with emotion.

Eleanor shook her head slowly. "Not after that summer. Circumstances pulled us apart." She didn't elaborate, and Annabell knew better than to press. Whatever had happened, it was clear that the memory still held her captive, both a source of joy and a wound that had never fully healed.

Annabell felt a deep sadness settle over her. She wanted to comfort her Nana, to tell her that love, no matter how fleeting, was still worth cherishing. But she didn't know how. Instead, she walked over and wrapped her arms around Eleanor, holding her tightly.

For a moment, neither of them spoke. They simply stood there, two generations bound by the weight of unspoken words and shared wonder at the stories only time could tell.

Chapter 3

The room was quiet except for the faint hum of the city that never slept. The amber glow of the lamps painted soft shadows across the walls of Suite 56, and from the open window came the distant echo of a saxophone drifting up from the street below a sound that seemed to wrap itself around Nana Eleanor like a ghost from her past.

She sat by the window again, her frail hands resting on the carved wooden sill, the veins along her skin catching the faint light. Her gaze, distant and unfocused, was somewhere far beyond the glittering skyline of New York. The years had melted away.

Annabell, sitting across from her with a cup of tea cooling untouched between her hands, watched her grandmother in silence. There was something in Nana's eyes that both frightened and fascinated her a kind of depth she'd never seen before, as if all the love and sorrow of a lifetime were quietly resurfacing.

Finally, Annabell spoke, her voice gentle, almost afraid to disturb the fragile stillness.

"Nana," she whispered, "did you love him?"

The question seemed to pull Eleanor back to the present. She turned slowly, her expression soft but haunted. "Did I love him?" she repeated quietly, tasting the words like something sacred. "Oh, my dear... I loved him in ways I didn't even understand back then. He was my first thought in the morning, my last thought before sleep. When I heard his music, it was as though he could see straight into my soul."

Annabell leaned forward, her heart tightening. "What happened to him?" she asked softly, though she could already sense the ache that lay behind the question.

Eleanor drew in a trembling breath and turned her gaze back to the city lights. "We were worlds apart, Annabell," she said finally. "Our families... our states... even our very names drew lines between us. He came from nothing. His parents ran a small bar in Chicago, and he played piano from the time he could reach the keys. I came from old money and expectations that pressed down like iron. To my parents, Henry was a dalliance at best a scandal waiting to unfold."

She paused, her voice trembling with both anger and sorrow. "But to me, he was freedom."

Annabell could almost see it her young Nana in her youth, filled with wild laughter and defiant hope, meeting Henry under glittering chandeliers and moonlit skies. "Did you meet in secret?" she asked, barely above a whisper.

Eleanor nodded, her eyes glistening. "Always. The first time, it was by accident. I'd slipped away from one of Aunt Agatha's tedious dinners to escape the endless talk of propriety and

marriage prospects. I wandered into the lounge and there he was, sitting at the piano, playing something so beautiful it made me forget where I was. His fingers danced across the keys like silk, and the room fell away. When he looked up at me, I swear time stopped."

Her voice softened, filled with wonder. "He smiled that kind of smile that reaches right through you, as if he already knew your secrets. I couldn't move. Couldn't speak. He simply said, 'You look like someone who belongs in music, not in silence.'"

Annabell smiled faintly, her throat tightening. "That's beautiful."

Eleanor gave a small nod, a sad smile touching her lips. "It was the beginning. From that night on, we met whenever we could. In the rose gardens behind the hotel, on the balcony after midnight, sometimes even down by the piano when no one was listening. We'd talk for hours — about dreams, about what life could be if the world were kinder. He wanted to travel, to play in Paris, to see the world. And I... I wanted to be brave enough to go with him."

She fell silent then, her eyes clouding with the weight of memory. "But the world had other plans."

Annabell's heart ached. "They found out?"

Eleanor nodded, her jaw tightening. "My father caught wind of it. He said I was bringing shame to the family name. My mother pleaded with me to end it, to 'think of my future.' As if my future could exist without him." Her voice broke on the last word. "Henry begged me to run away said we could go anywhere, start over. He even bought two train tickets, first to Chicago, then on to California. He was so sure we could make it."

Annabell could see the tears in her Nana's eyes now, the years of regret that had never truly faded. "But you didn't go," she whispered.

"No," Eleanor breathed. "I was a coward. I was sixteen, bound by duty and fear. I told him I couldn't. That I wouldn't. The words tasted like poison even as I said them. I'll never forget the look in his eyes, not anger, not even disappointment... just sorrow. The kind that stays with you forever."

The silence that followed was heavy, filled with all the things that had gone unsaid.

Annabell reached across and took her grandmother's trembling hands in her own. "You were so young, Nana. You didn't have the power then."

Eleanor's eyes lifted, glistening. "Perhaps. But the choice was still mine. And I made the wrong one." She drew a long breath, her gaze drifting back toward the skyline. "The morning after I told him goodbye, he left the Waldorf. I never saw him again. No note. No message. Just the echo of the piano he used to play. It was like the music itself had died with him."

Annabell felt tears slide down her own cheeks now. "Did you ever try to find him?"

"I thought about it," Eleanor admitted. "Many times. But pride... pride is a terrible thing. I told myself he'd moved on, that I should too. But I never really did. I married your grandfather later, of course. He was kind. Dependable. But he never made my heart race the way Henry did. Even now, when I close my eyes, I can still hear the melody he played that last night — the song he wrote for me. I've carried it with me all these years."

She smiled faintly, though her eyes shimmered with tears. "He told me it was called 'Eleanor's Waltz.' I've never heard it since."

Annabell's heart swelled with empathy and a strange, aching admiration. To have loved so deeply, to have carried that love across a lifetime it both broke and inspired her.

"Nana," she said softly, "what if that's why you came back here? Maybe you weren't just revisiting the past. Maybe... maybe you were hoping to find him again."

Eleanor looked at her granddaughter, the faintest glimmer of hope flickering in her tired eyes. "I don't know, my dear. Perhaps I was. Perhaps some part of me never stopped waiting."

Annabell squeezed her hand gently. "Then maybe it's not too late."

Eleanor let out a trembling breath. "Oh, Annabell... I wouldn't even know where to start. It's been nearly seventy years. He could be anywhere or nowhere."

But even as she said the words, something in her heart stirred something warm and alive. The thought that Henry's melody might still linger somewhere in this city, waiting to be heard, made her chest ache in a way that was almost sweet.

Annabell smiled through her tears. "We'll find him, Nana. Or at least, we'll find his story. Together."

For a long moment, neither of them spoke. The city below shimmered like a sea of stars, and the wind carried faint strains of a piano from somewhere in the distance, soft, hesitant, but unmistakably real.

Eleanor froze. Her breath hitched.

"Do you hear that?" she whispered.

Annabell turned toward the window. The melody was faint, but it was there a waltz, slow and haunting, drifting up from the lobby below.

Eleanor pressed a trembling hand to her lips, her eyes filling once more. "It can't be..."

But in her heart in the depths of her soul she knew that song. Eleanor's Waltz.

Chapter 4

For a moment, the world stood still.

Eleanor's frail hand trembled against the glass as the melody drifted through the night air faint, ghostlike, yet unmistakable. The opening notes of Eleanor's Waltz wove their way through the silence like a whisper from another lifetime. Each sound carried the weight of decades, and with every measure, her heart tightened, as if it recognized something her mind could not yet accept.

Annabell's eyes widened. She had never seen her Nana look like this transfixed, breathless, caught somewhere between disbelief and hope. "Nana?" she said softly. "What is it?"

Eleanor's lips parted, her voice little more than air, "That song... I know that song."

Annabell frowned, "You mean?"

"It's his song," Eleanor breathed, her eyes glistening with tears. "It's Henry's."

Without another word, she rose slowly, painfully her hand gripping her walking stick, the tremor in her limbs matched only by the pounding of her heart. Annabell instinctively reached to steady her, but Eleanor waved her off, her gaze fixed on the door. "Help me to the lobby," she said, her voice fragile yet certain. "Please."

The two of them moved through the quiet hallway, the carpet muffling their hurried footsteps. The elevator chimed softly, its golden doors sliding open to reveal a reflection of two women — one young, one old, bound together by love and destiny.

As the elevator descended, Eleanor's thoughts whirled like autumn leaves caught in a storm. It couldn't be him. Not after all this time. Yet every note of that melody seemed to reach into her chest and stir something she thought had long been buried. Could it be that fate, in its strange cruelty and beauty, had brought her back here for a reason?

When the doors opened onto the lobby, time seemed to blur. The space was dimly lit, the chandeliers above casting soft halos of golden light. The air was thick with the scent of polished wood and aged bourbon. There near the corner of the room, beside the grand piano the music continued.

The pianist was an older man, his posture proud yet softened by age. His hair was silver, his back slightly hunched, but his hands... his hands were sure and graceful as they danced across the keys.

Eleanor stopped mid-step. Her breath caught in her throat.

Annabell turned to her, alarmed by the sudden stillness. "Nana?"

Eleanor's eyes filled, her voice a trembling whisper. "Those hands... I'd know them anywhere."

The pianist finished the piece with a soft, lingering chord, the sound fading into the hush of the lobby. For a heartbeat, there was silence the kind that feels alive, humming with everything unsaid. Then he looked up.

Their eyes met.

In that instant, seventy years fell away.

The noise of the world the faint chatter of the night staff, the distant clatter of glasses melted into nothing. All that existed were those eyes, still bright, still warm, still achingly familiar.

"Eleanor?" His voice cracked like old parchment, yet her name carried the same tenderness it always had.

Her hand flew to her mouth. "Henry..."

Annabell froze, staring between them in disbelief. She had expected to find a memory, a story — not a living, breathing piece of the past. The air around them felt charged, sacred.

Henry rose slowly from the piano bench, his movements hesitant, as though afraid she might vanish if he came too close. "I didn't think I'd ever see you again," he said, his voice low and thick with emotion. "Not here. Not after all this time."

Eleanor took a shaky step forward. "I never thought I would either," she whispered. "But I heard the song... and I knew. I always knew."

Henry gave a soft, incredulous laugh, one that carried both joy and sorrow. "I never stopped playing it," he said. "Not once. I played it in every city, every place I went. It was the only thing that still felt like home."

Annabell pressed a hand to her chest, her heart aching at the sight of them — two souls bound by a melody that had outlasted everything else.

Eleanor closed the distance between them, her steps slow but sure. When she finally reached him, she lifted a trembling hand to his cheek. The warmth of his skin beneath her fingertips sent tears spilling down her face. "You're really here," she whispered, half to herself.

Henry covered her hand with his own, his grip strong despite the years. "I never left," he said softly. "Not truly. Every time I played, I saw you sitting there in that blue dress, smiling like you were the only one in the room. I thought maybe one day, if I played long enough, you'd find your way back."

Her breath hitched. "Oh, Henry... I was so afraid. I told myself I was doing what was right, but I've regretted it every day since."

He shook his head gently. "No regrets, Ellie. We were just young. The world wasn't ready for us then."

"But it might be now," Annabell said suddenly, her voice trembling. Both of them turned toward her, the faintest smile on Henry's lips. "Maybe this time, the world will let you finish your story."

Eleanor looked at her granddaughter, then back at Henry. For a moment, none of them spoke. The years, the pain, the missed chances it all hung there between them, fragile and luminous.

Henry stepped back toward the piano, his hand gesturing toward the seat beside him. "Dance with me," he said softly. "Just once more. For old time's sake."

Eleanor's eyes widened, a soft laugh escaping her lips. "Henry, I can hardly walk without this stick."

"Then lean on me," he said with a smile that melted her heart. "You did once before."

Annabell watched through blurred vision as her grandmother took his arm, her frail frame trembling but alive with purpose. Henry began to play again, the notes slow and tender, echoing through the quiet hall. Eleanor closed her eyes, letting the music carry her back to that long-ago night the one when the world was wide, and love was new, and everything still felt possible.

For Annabell, it was like watching a dream come to life not just her Nana's, but a reminder that love, real love, never truly dies. It waits, patient and unyielding, until time itself folds back to make room for it once more.

When the final note lingered in the air, Henry looked up at her and whispered, "You were always my song, Ellie."

In that instant surrounded by the soft light of the past and the promise of forgiveness Eleanor finally let go of seventy years of regret.

She smiled through her tears and whispered back, "And you were my heart."

Chapter 5

Morning arrived softly over New York, the golden light filtering through the high windows of the Waldorf Astoria like a blessing. The first hum of the city stirred below — the distant whir of traffic, the rhythm of footsteps on the sidewalks, the occasional honk from a taxi weaving through the morning rush. The city was waking up, alive and unstoppable, yet inside Suite 56, time seemed to move at a gentler pace.

The scent of coffee drifted from a silver pot on the small table near the window. Annabell stood beside it, still in her robe, her hair tousled from sleep. She had barely slept at all. The events of the previous night had played over and over in her mind the melody, the reunion, the tears in her Nana's eyes, and the soft warmth of Henry's voice calling her "Ellie."

She looked over at her grandmother now. Eleanor sat by the window again, the morning light washing over her face and softening the lines that time had carved. There was a calmness about her, a quiet glow that Annabell hadn't seen in years perhaps ever. Her Nana's eyes, though tired, carried a spark that was unmistakably alive.

Annabell approached quietly, "You look peaceful this morning," she said, setting down two cups of coffee on the table.

Eleanor smiled faintly. "I feel... lighter," she admitted. "For the first time in decades, I slept without the weight of what-ifs pressing on my heart."

Annabell sat opposite her, curling her legs under the chair. "It still feels unreal," she said softly, "Seeing him hearing that song. It was like something out of a dream."

Eleanor's smile deepened, wistful yet tender. "It felt like a dream to me too, darling. But it was real. He was real." She sighed, her gaze drifting toward the window. "And to think, all this time, he's been here. Playing. Remembering."

Annabell hesitated, then asked the question that had been pressing on her mind all night. "Did you talk more after I left you two alone?"

Eleanor nodded, a soft sadness flickering across her face. "Yes. We talked until nearly dawn."

She paused, taking a long sip of her coffee before continuing. "He never married," she said quietly. "He said there was never anyone else he wanted to share his music with. After I left, he went back to Chicago for a time, played in small clubs, then moved around New Orleans, Paris, London. He made a name for himself as a composer, but he never took credit for one piece."

Annabell frowned, "Which piece?"

Eleanor's eyes softened. "Eleanor's Waltz. He never published it under his own name. Said it belonged to someone else to the girl who never got to hear it played under the stars the way he'd intended."

Annabell felt her chest tighten. "He meant you."

Eleanor nodded, her voice trembling. "He said the song was his promise that one day, when the time was right, it would find its way back to me. And it did. Last night, when I heard it, I thought I was dreaming. But when I saw him..." Her voice faltered, tears gathering again. "Oh, Annabell. I never believed the world could be so kind."

Annabell reached across the table and took her grandmother's hand. "Maybe it's not kindness," she said softly. "Maybe it's fate finally keeping its promise."

They sat in silence for a moment, the quiet hum of the city beneath them filling the spaces between their words. Sunlight spilled across the room, catching the gold embroidery of the curtains and reflecting off the glass frames that lined the walls. Outside, the city shimmered like a living memory vibrant, unending, beautiful in its imperfection.

Eleanor smiled faintly as she looked out the window. "You know, Henry told me something before I left him last night."

"What was it?" Annabell asked.

"He said that every note of Eleanor's Waltz was written from memory not of what we were, but of what we could have been. He said he wrote it the night after I told him goodbye." Her eyes glistened with fresh tears.

"He said he never changed a single note because that's how he remembered me unfinished, but beautiful all the same."

Annabell's breath caught. "That's... heartbreakingly lovely."

Eleanor smiled, though her voice trembled. "He said he'd kept playing it, not out of sadness, but because it reminded him that even brief love, love that ends can still be real. That it can shape who we are long after it's gone."

Annabell felt tears prick her eyes. "Nana, that's..." She stopped, her voice breaking. "That's everything love is supposed to be."

For a while, they said nothing. The air between them was heavy with emotion, but also with something gentle acceptance, understanding, peace.

Then Eleanor looked toward the door, a new thought lighting in her expression. "He invited us to his performance tonight," she said softly. "He plays every Thursday in the hotel's ballroom it's where we first met."

Annabell smiled, her heart swelling. "Then we'll be there."

The rest of the morning passed quietly. Eleanor took her time getting ready, her movements slower than they once were, but with a grace that Annabell found captivating. The room filled with the faint scent of her favourite rosewater perfume, and as she pinned her silver hair in its familiar bun, Annabell caught herself imagining the young woman her grandmother once was the one who had danced beneath chandeliers and whispered promises under the moonlight.

As the morning light gave way to the soft haze of afternoon, Annabell felt something shift within her. Seeing her Nana's love story come back to life had awakened something in her own heart a hope she hadn't realized she'd been missing.

She looked at her grandmother, now sitting once again by the window, her eyes alight with quiet antici-pation.

"Do you think love like that still exists?" Annabell asked.

Eleanor turned her head and smiled. "Oh, my dear, love never disappears. It changes, it hides, sometimes it waits longer than it should... but it's always there. You just have to be brave enough to listen for it like I did last night."

Annabell looked out at the city below the steady pulse of New York, full of stories, chances, and fleeting connections. Maybe her Nana was right. Maybe love didn't die; it only lingered, waiting for the right moment to return.

As the day slowly faded into evening, the Waldorf Astoria began to glow once more with golden light. The faint hum of laughter and the clinking of glasses echoed from the grand hall below.

Somewhere, drifting upward through the corridors, the first soft notes of a piano began again familiar, tender, full of promise.

Eleanor smiled. "He's started."

Annabell took her hand. "Then let's not keep him waiting."

They rose together one with a lifetime behind her, one with all her life still ahead as they walked toward the door, Annabell felt it: that subtle, unshakable truth that love, like music, never truly ends.

It simply finds a new way to begin again.

Chapter 6

The evening air was velvet-soft, carrying with it the faint perfume of the flowers arranged throughout the Waldorf Astoria's grand ballroom. Chandeliers dripped with golden light, casting warm reflections across marble floors and satin gowns. The murmur of conversation and the low clinking of champagne flutes filled the space with a hum of anticipation, but for Eleanor, all of it faded to a distant blur.

She stood just beyond the ballroom entrance, her hand resting on Annabell's arm for balance. The scent of polished oak, wax candles, and nostalgia seemed to wrap around her like a memory made tangible.

"Are you sure you're ready, Nana?" Annabell asked softly.

Eleanor gave a small smile fragile yet resolute. "I've waited a lifetime for this moment, my dear. I don't think I could bear to wait another day."

The maître d' led them to a table near the front, close enough to the piano that Eleanor could see the fine detailing of its mahogany body. The instrument gleamed under the soft light, its lid open, awaiting its player. As they sat, Annabell noticed her Nana's trembling hands and placed hers gently over them.

Eleanor's gaze swept across the room, and for a fleeting instant, she was sixteen again dressed in blue satin, laughter spilling from her lips as she slipped away from Aunt Agatha's watchful eye. The world had been new then, full of light and possibility. And now, here she was, older, slower, but still carrying that same beating heart.

The murmuring crowd quieted as Henry stepped onto the stage.

Time had left its traces on him silver in his hair, fine lines etched around his eyes but to Eleanor, he looked unchanged. There was still that same steadiness in his stance, that same quiet strength. He wore a black suit, perfectly pressed, but his eyes, when they met hers, were what made her breath catch. They held that familiar warmth, that spark of mischief and tenderness that had once set her world alight.

"Good evening," Henry said, his voice carrying easily through the room. "Tonight's performance is... something I've been waiting to play for many years. A piece written a lifetime ago, for someone I never forgot."

Eleanor's breath trembled.

Henry's gaze lingered on her for a moment longer before he turned to the piano. As he sat and let his fingers rest upon the keys, a hush fell over the ballroom.

The first note was soft barely more than a whisper and yet it filled the space as if the walls themselves remembered.

Eleanor's Waltz.

The melody unfolded like a story being retold after decades of silence. It began tenderly, with the gentleness of first love notes that brushed against one another like the touch of shy hands meeting in secret. Then the rhythm swelled, blooming into something full and breathtaking a sound that captured youth's boundless joy and daring.

Eleanor's eyes glistened as the music carried her back. She saw herself again beneath the chandeliers of 1946, laughing as Henry spun her across the marble floor. She felt the thrill of his hand at her waist, the unspoken promise in his gaze. She felt everything she thought time had stolen returned to her through each rise and fall of the melody.

Annabell, sitting beside her, felt the tears come unbidden. The music seemed to reach inside her chest, touching something deep and universal the ache of love remembered, of choices made, of time that could never be regained but could still be cherished. She glanced at her grandmother and was struck by the look of serenity on her face. Eleanor's lips moved silently, as though she were speaking to the music itself.

When the waltz reached its center the heartbeat of the piece Henry paused, his hands hovering above the keys. The audience held its breath. Then, softly, he spoke.

"There's a part of this story no one ever knew," he said quietly, his eyes never leaving Eleanor. "When I first wrote this piece, I wrote it for her. But over the years, I realized it wasn't just hers. It belonged to everyone who ever loved and lost, who ever made a choice they wished they could undo, and who ever found the courage to forgive themselves."

Eleanor pressed a trembling hand to her heart.

Henry's fingers touched the keys again but this time, the music changed. It deepened, softened, evolved. A new movement one that Eleanor had never heard before unfurled into the air.

Annabell leaned closer, her heart racing. "Nana... this part wasn't there before, was it?"

Eleanor shook her head slowly, her eyes fixed on Henry. "No," she whispered. "This is new."

As the notes rose and fell, something within her shifted. This was not a lament for what had been lost, but a hymn for what had endured. The melody spoke of forgiveness, of time reclaimed, of love that transcended the years that separated them.

And then she understood.

This was Henry's final gesture not an ending, but a completion. The song that had once been unfinished had found its missing verse.

Her tears came freely now, but they were not born of sorrow. They were tears of release, of gratitude.

When the last note lingered in the air, the room fell utterly silent. Henry lifted his hands slowly from the keys, his gaze meeting Eleanor's once more. The applause began softly hesitant, reverent then swelled into a wave that filled the ballroom.

But Eleanor didn't hear it. She was lost in that gaze, in the quiet conversation that passed between them without words.

Annabell turned to her Nana and felt a lump rise in her throat. She could almost see it the invisible thread that stretched across time, pulling two souls back together until nothing stood between them anymore.

Henry rose from the piano bench and made his way toward their table. The applause faded as people stepped aside, sensing something sacred in the moment. When he reached Eleanor, he extended his hand just as he had so many years before.

"Ellie," he said softly, "may I have this dance?"

A hush fell over the room again.

Eleanor's lips curved into a trembling smile. "After seventy years," she whispered, "I thought you'd never ask."

The crowd watched in silent reverence as she rose, leaning lightly on his arm. Together, they moved slow, delicate, but beautiful. The pianist behind them resumed Eleanor's Waltz, its notes floating through the air like a benediction.

Annabell watched with tears streaming down her face, her heart full to bursting. Around her, the world seemed to shimmer the golden light, the music, the weight of memory and grace. She realized then that love's truest legacy wasn't the story itself, but the way it changed those who bore witness to it.

When the final chord faded, Henry drew Eleanor close. "You were my music," he murmured.

"And you," she replied through a trembling smile, "were my forever."

The room erupted in gentle applause once more, though the sound felt distant, like the closing of a curtain on a story that had finally found its peace.

That night, as Annabell helped her Nana back to their suite, the air was still warm with music. The city beyond the window pulsed with life headlights gleaming like tiny constellations scattered across the streets. Eleanor sat for a long time in silence, her eyes reflecting both joy and finality.

Annabell sat beside her, holding her hand. "You found him," she whispered.

Eleanor smiled faintly, her voice barely audible. "No, darling... he found me. Again."

Somewhere, faint but clear, the melody of Eleanor's Waltz drifted through the night once more not a song of longing, but of completion.

For Eleanor, it was the sound of peace, for Annabell, it was the sound of hope a reminder that love, once found, never truly fades. It simply changes form and plays on.

Chapter 7

The next few days unfolded like pages from a dream that neither Eleanor nor Annabell wanted to end.

New York glowed beneath a veil of late summer sunlight, its skyline a mosaic of glass and gold. The Waldorf Astoria, grand and eternal, seemed to hum with unseen energy as if the very walls remembered the night of the waltz and refused to let it fade.

Eleanor spent her mornings by the same window in Suite 56, watching the city move with the rhythm of a heartbeat she had once thought lost. Each sunrise seemed to paint her in light, soft and golden, and Annabell often found herself pausing just to take in the sight of her peaceful, whole, radiant in a way she hadn't been for decades.

Henry visited them each day, sometimes bringing fresh lilies from the florist down the street Eleanor's favourite. He would sit across from her with coffee in hand, and together they would talk for hours. Their conversations were gentle, unhurried about music, about lost years, about forgiveness. Occasionally, Henry would reach over and brush her hand with his fingers, and that small gesture seemed to hold everything they had ever needed to say.

Annabell often sat quietly nearby, pretending to read, but really, she just listened. She was captivated by the tenderness that passed between them — the easy silences, the laughter that sounded like something reborn. She couldn't help but think that love like theirs was rare not the kind that burned bright and vanished, but the kind that lingered like a melody that refuses to end.

The air inside the suite felt different now. Lighter. As though something sacred had shifted a lifetime of grief lifted, leaving only peace in its place.

One evening, as the sun dipped low over the skyline, Henry came to the suite with a small box tucked beneath his arm. His eyes sparkled with quiet excitement. "I've something to give you both," he said as he set it on the table.

Eleanor tilted her head, smiling, "Henry, you've given me enough simply by being here."

He chuckled softly, "Humour me."

Inside the box lay a record the label worn, the writing faint but legible. Eleanor's Waltz – Henry Dalton.

Annabell's eyes widened. "You recorded it?"

Henry nodded. "A long time ago. I kept one copy for myself, never released it publicly. I wasn't ready for the world to hear it. But now..." His gaze shifted to Eleanor, "Now I think it belongs to her and to you, Annabell. It's your family's story now."

Eleanor reached for the record, her fingers tracing the grooves of the label. "You kept it all these years," she murmured.

"I told you," Henry said gently. "Some melodies never leave us."

Annabell felt her chest tighten as she looked between them. She knew she was witnessing the closing of something precious but also the beginning of something else entirely.

Later that night, they played the record on the old gramophone the hotel staff had brought up for them. As the needle touched the vinyl, the soft crackle gave way to the tender sweep of the waltz. The room filled with sound warm, deep, timeless.

Eleanor sat back in her chair, eyes closed, a faint smile on her lips. Henry's hand rested over hers, their fingers intertwined.

Annabell stood by the window, watching the city lights blink awake. Tears slipped down her cheeks, but she didn't wipe them away. She let them fall quietly, freely because they weren't tears of sadness. They were of gratitude.

In that moment, she understood something profound: love, when true, doesn't end. It changes shape. It becomes part of everything the light, the air, the music that carries on long after the players are gone.

The following morning, the air was unusually still. The city's pulse seemed softer, the light more subdued. Annabell woke to the faint sound of the gramophone still spinning, the record's edge clicking gently as it reached its end. She rose and crossed the room, her heart heavy with the quiet.

Eleanor was still in her chair by the window, the morning light painting her in gold. Her expression was peaceful, her hands folded lightly in her lap, Henry's record resting beside her. She looked almost as though she had simply drifted into sleep her features serene, her spirit free.

Annabell felt her breath catch, a wave of emotion crashing through her chest. Tears blurred her vision as she knelt beside her grandmother, taking her cool hand into her own. "Oh, Nana..." she whispered, her voice trembling. "You found your forever."

Through her grief, she smiled. There was no tragedy in this moment only completion. Her grandmother had lived long enough to reclaim the love she lost, to hear her song again, and to leave the world with her heart full.

Henry came later that morning. When he saw Eleanor, he didn't speak. He simply knelt beside her, took her hand, and pressed it to his lips. The tears that fell down his cheeks were silent, but his eyes full of love and peace said everything.

Annabell stepped away to the window, giving them their last moment together. Outside, the world went on sunlight shimmering off car roofs, people hurrying along the sidewalks, the faint music of a saxophone drifting from somewhere below. Life continued, as it always did, carrying echoes of the stories it had witnessed.

In the days that followed, the Waldorf seemed to hold its breath. The staff who had grown fond of Eleanor spoke of her with quiet reverence. Guests passing through the lobby sometimes paused by the piano, where a single white lily rested on its lid, placed there by Henry each morning.

Annabell stayed for another week, unable to leave yet unwilling to let grief darken what had been so beautiful. She spent her mornings in the suite, writing in her journal not about loss, but about love, memory, and music. At night, she'd wander down to the ballroom, where Henry still played.

But one evening, when she arrived, the piano was empty. Only the faint sound of a recorded waltz played through the hotel speakers Eleanor's Waltz. On the piano bench lay a letter, sealed in a simple white envelope.

It was addressed to her.

My dear Annabell,

If you are reading this, then I have gone to join her as I always knew I would.

Do not let sadness take root in your heart. We had our ending, and it was perfect. The music lives on now in you in your courage, your compassion, and the way you see the world.

Remember this: love, true love, is never lost. It is only passed on, like a song from one generation to the next.

Play it when you need to remember us. And when you find your own great love, play it then too so that we might dance once more.

With all my heart,

Henry

Annabell's tears fell freely as she read the letter. Her heart ached, yet there was warmth beneath the sorrow a fullness that spoke of completion.

That night, she sat at the piano for the first time. The room was empty, save for the gentle glow of candlelight. Her fingers trembled as they hovered over the keys, then pressed softly into the opening notes.

The melody rose, delicate and pure Eleanor's Waltz reborn.

It filled the ballroom, wrapped around the chandeliers, drifted up the stairwell, and out into the New York night. For anyone listening, it was simply a beautiful song. But for Annabell, it was everything a promise, a farewell, a beginning.

As she played, she imagined them her Nana and Henry dancing together once more in some place where time could no longer separate them. The music carried her tears, her love, her gratitude. And when the last note faded, she sat in silence, smiling through her grief.

Outside, dawn began to rise. The first light spilled across the marble floor, catching on the polished wood of the piano. The world, for a heartbeat, felt utterly still.

Annabell whispered into the quiet, "I'll keep it alive, Nana. I promise."

And with that, she knew the story wasn't ending.

It was beginning again not in sorrow, but in legacy. In love, a waltz that would echo forever through the passage of time.

Chapter 8

Two Years Later – The Waldorf Astoria, New York

The taxi turned the final corner, and the Waldorf Astoria came into view timeless, majestic, shimmering beneath the spring rain that slicked the pavement in sheets of silver.

Annabell leaned forward, her heart tightening as the grand façade rose before her. Two years. Two years since she'd walked through those revolving doors. Two years since her grandmother had passed peacefully in the suite that overlooked the city skyline. Two years since she had heard Eleanor's Waltz played live for the last time.

The driver pulled up to the curb. Annabell hesitated before stepping out, glancing up at the hotel's façade its soft amber lights glowing against the dusk. The sight was like stepping back into another life.

She had come to New York for a reason.

The Museum of American Music had invited her to speak at the unveiling of a new exhibit "Timeless Love: The Life and Music of Henry Dalton." They had restored his recordings, including Eleanor's Waltz, and were dedicating the collection to both him and the woman who had inspired it. The program listed them together: Henry Dalton and Eleanor Thourpe — A Love Across Time.

Annabell had accepted the invitation immediately, knowing she had to be here. It wasn't just for the museum. It was for them.

Inside the hotel, the lobby was just as she remembered polished marble floors gleaming under soft golden light, the faint hum of conversation echoing beneath crystal chandeliers. Everything smelled faintly of roses and aged wood polish. The same piano still stood in the corner of the room, its surface buffed to a shine, a single white lily resting on its lid.

Her breath caught.

It was the same kind Henry had left there every morning after Eleanor passed. The tradition, she realized, had continued perhaps kept alive by someone who remembered, or by the hotel itself, which seemed to hold the memory of its guests like gentle ghosts.

At the reception desk, the clerk smiled warmly. "Welcome back to the Waldorf, Miss Chappelle. We have you in Suite Fifty-Six, as requested."

Annabell's chest tightened. The same room. The one where it had all happened.

As she took the elevator up, the soft instrumental music playing through the speakers felt eerily familiar. The air carried that same blend of history and quiet reverence the sense that time, somehow, was folding in on itself again.

When the doors opened, she stepped into the hallway, her heels clicking softly on the patterned carpet. The door to Suite 56 waited at the end, just as it had before. Her hand trembled as she slid the keycard through the lock and pushed the door open.

The scent hit her first a faint trace of rosewater and lilies. She froze. The room looked almost untouched, as though time had paused here the day Eleanor and Henry last sat by the window. The same antique furniture gleamed softly in the evening light, the same pale curtains billowed in the breeze from the open window.

She set her suitcase down quietly and crossed to the window. The skyline stretched before her dazzling, infinite. The city was alive, pulsing with stories, with music, with memory.

Her throat tightened as she whispered, "I'm back, Nana."

For a long while, she simply stood there, listening to the faint hum of the city below taxis, laughter, footsteps, life. Then, from somewhere far down in the lobby, a piano began to play.

Her heart stilled.

The notes floated upward, delicate and slow Eleanor's Waltz.

But it was different.

There was something fresh in it a subtle variation, like a conversation between past and present. Someone had reinterpreted it. The melody carried both the weight of memory and the shimmer of renewal.

Annabell pressed her hand to her lips, tears rising in her eyes. "Someone's still playing it..."

Drawn by the sound, she left the room and descended the grand staircase, her pulse quickening with every step. The closer she came, the clearer the music became fluid, emotional, alive.

When she reached the edge of the lobby, she saw him.

A man perhaps in his early thirties sat at the piano. His hair was dark and slightly unruly, his posture relaxed but focused, his eyes closed as he played. He wasn't reading sheet music; he played as though he knew it by heart.

Annabell stood perfectly still, the melody wrapping around her like silk. For a moment, she wasn't sure if she was hearing Henry again through time, or if fate mischievous and poetic as ever had sent someone new to remind her that stories, like songs, never truly end.

When he finished, he opened his eyes and saw her standing there.

He smiled. "Beautiful piece, isn't it?"

Annabell swallowed, her voice catching. "It's... more than that. It's a story."

He tilted his head, intrigued. "You know it?"

She nodded slowly. "It was written for my grandmother."

Recognition flickered in his eyes. "You're Annabell Thorpe."

Her breath caught. "You know who I am?"

"I should," he said with a smile. "I'm the curator for the Dalton exhibit. I've been studying his compositions for years. I actually restored the master recording of Eleanor's Waltz. It's an extraordinary piece but I've always wondered about the woman behind it."

Annabell smiled softly, her eyes glistening. "She was extraordinary too."

They talked for a long time after that about Henry, about Eleanor, about music, about how love could be both fleeting and infinite. His name was Elias, he spoke of music the same way Henry once had not as sound, but as feeling, as truth.

As the night deepened, and the hotel grew quieter, Elias turned back to the piano. "Would you play it with me?" he asked gently.

Annabell hesitated, then nodded. Together, they sat two strangers bound by a melody born long before their time. Their hands brushed as they began to play. The music flowed, weaving the past and present into something seamless, timeless, alive.

And as the final note lingered, Annabell felt it the presence of her Nana, faint but certain, like the warmth of a hand resting gently on her shoulder.

She smiled through her tears.

Because she knew truly knew that this was not an ending.

It was another beginning.

Chapter 9

The following evening unfolded like a dream Annabell didn't want to wake from.

The Waldorf's ballroom, restored and softly lit for the Dalton Exhibition Gala, shimmered beneath chandeliers of crystal and gold. The air was fragrant with lilies and warmed by the hum of anticipation from guests who had come to celebrate the man whose music had become legend.

At the edge of the room, Annabell Thorpe stood beside Elias, her heart caught between the elegance of the moment and the quiet thrum of something she couldn't yet name.

He looked different tonight dressed in a black tuxedo, his normally tousled hair brushed neatly back. Yet, when he smiled, there was that same spark of warmth that had struck her the night before, when his hands had moved across the piano keys like they'd known the song all their lives.

Around them, the hotel pulsed with soft nostalgia velvet curtains drawn high, glasses clinking in polite conversation, the scent of wax candles blending with faint notes of champagne and perfume. It all felt suspended in time, a careful echo of the nights her grandmother once knew.

Annabell's gaze lingered on the stage where Henry's original grand piano stood. Its polished surface reflected the chandelier's golden light, and a single white lily rested atop it — just as it always had.

She felt her throat tighten. Nana would have loved this.

Elias noticed her quietness. "You're thinking of her," he said softly.

She nodded, blinking back a sudden rush of emotion. "Always. I think she'd be laughing right now — seeing me standing here, at a gala honouring Henry, with someone who loves his music as much as she did."

He smiled gently. "She'd be proud of you. You've kept their story alive."

Annabell looked down at the program in her hands — Henry Dalton: The Eternal Waltz — A Night in Celebration of Love and Legacy. Beneath the title, her name appeared as Guest Speaker: Annabell Thorpe, granddaughter of Eleanor Thorpe — muse of Henry Dalton.

Muse. The word carried both beauty and ache.

"She was more than his muse," Annabell said after a moment, her voice low. "She was his heart. And for so long, she thought she'd lost him. But the truth was, she'd lived inside his music all along. That's why I'm here, Elias not just to speak, but to remind people that their story wasn't about loss. It was about time... and how love defies it."

Elias studied her for a moment, admiration flickering in his eyes. "You sound like someone who's lived the story herself."

Annabell gave a small, wistful smile. "Maybe I have."

Before he could answer, the lights dimmed. The room quieted as the master of ceremonies took the stage, his voice carrying through the microphone with measured grace.

"Ladies and gentlemen, tonight we celebrate a man whose music transcended generations Henry Dalton. His melodies spoke of longing, of memory, of love that endures beyond the passage of years. And tonight, we are honoured to welcome Miss Annabell Thorpe, whose grandmother, Eleanor, inspired his most beloved piece — Eleanor's Waltz."

Applause rose softly, filling the ballroom like a wave. Annabell drew in a breath and stepped toward the podium, her heels tapping against the marble floor.

As she stood before the crowd, the lights glimmered against the crystal chandeliers above, and for a brief second, she thought she saw her grandmother's reflection among them — poised, smiling, radiant.

"My grandmother used to tell me," Annabell began, her voice steady but gentle, "that music doesn't just belong to the past. It's a living thing it carries every emotion, every heartbeat of those who loved before us. Henry's music isn't just history. It's a memory that breathes."

She paused, her gaze drifting to the piano. "I came back here tonight because I wanted to stand where they stood — where love first found its melody, and where it came full circle decades later. Their story isn't a tragedy. It's a testament that even when the world tries to separate two hearts, music will always find a way to bring them home."

The audience was silent, spellbound.

When she stepped down, Elias met her with a soft smile. "That was beautiful, Annabell. You spoke from your soul."

"I spoke from theirs," she whispered.

The rest of the evening passed in a blur of applause and conversation, but as the crowd began to thin and the music softened into a lingering piano piece, Elias turned to her.

"Would you walk with me?" he asked.

They slipped away from the ballroom, moving through the quiet corridors of the Waldorf. The air was cooler here, tinged with the scent of lilies and polished oak. As they reached the grand staircase, Annabell looked down into the now-empty lobby the same lobby where Eleanor had once stopped, breathless, at the sound of a familiar tune.

Elias leaned against the railing beside her. "It's strange, isn't it?" he said softly. "How places remember."

She nodded. "Yes. Sometimes I think the walls here still hum with their story."

A silence stretched between them gentle, comfortable. Then Elias spoke again, his voice almost hesitant. "When I restored Henry's recordings, I found something. A second version of Eleanor's Waltz. He'd never performed it publicly. It was labelled 'Eleanor's Waltz II — For the Future.' It had a new motif... something unfinished."

Annabell turned toward him, her heart suddenly quickening. "Unfinished?"

He nodded. "I think he wanted someone to finish it. Maybe not Eleanor maybe someone who carried her forward."

Their eyes met and, in that moment, Annabell understood what he meant.

"Play it with me," Elias said softly. "Tomorrow night. Here, in the ballroom. We'll finish it together."

Annabell's heart swelled a mix of nerves, awe, and something tender she hadn't felt in years. "I don't even know the ending."

He smiled faintly. "Maybe that's the point. Maybe it's for us to find."

Outside, rain began to fall soft, steady, rhythmic. The city lights shimmered through the droplets on the windows, turning New York into a sea of gold and silver reflections.

As they stood there, side by side, Annabell thought of her grandmother of that young girl in 1946 who had fallen in love with a pianist's song. She thought of the long years that had followed, the reunion, the peace, the melody that never died.

And she realized something that made her heart ache and soar all at once.

The waltz was never just Eleanor's.

It was hers too now.

That night, as she returned to Suite 56, she stood at the window, listening to the rain. The city pulsed below, alive and infinite. Somewhere deep within its hum, she swore she could hear faint strains of music a promise, carried forward through time.

She whispered into the quiet, "We'll finish it, Nana. I promise."

And from somewhere deep within her heart — or perhaps from somewhere far beyond she thought she heard the softest reply:

"Then dance, my darling. Dance."

Annabell closed her eyes, letting the sound of the city mingle with the melody that had lived in her family for generations. The waltz had begun anew not as remembrance, but as continuation.

Because love, once found, never ends. It simply changes hands and begins its song again.

Chapter 10

The Waltz Continues

The next evening, the Waldorf Astoria seemed to glow from within. The marble floors reflected soft golden light from chandeliers that swayed gently above the ballroom, their crystals scattering tiny prisms across the walls. The air was fragrant with lilies once more a quiet tribute to Eleanor and Henry, whose spirits seemed to linger in every note, every breath, every corner of the room.

Annabell Thorpe stood by the grand piano, her fingertips grazing its polished surface. It was the same piano Henry had once played the same instrument that had carried Eleanor's Waltz into the world. Tonight, it would sing again.

Elias stood beside her, sleeves rolled up, his dark hair slightly tousled in the way it always was when he was lost in thought. His expression was calm, but there was an energy beneath it something charged and alive. He looked at her with quiet reassurance.

"You ready?" he asked gently.

Annabell exhaled slowly, feeling her pulse quicken. "I don't think I'll ever really be ready," she admitted, her lips curving into a soft smile. "But I think she'd like that."

Elias returned her smile. "Then let's play for her."

The ballroom was empty except for a handful of hotel staff who had gathered discreetly at the edges the same staff who had watched Eleanor's reunion with Henry two years ago. They seemed to understand what this moment meant. The silence that filled the space was not expectation it was reverence.

Annabell sat beside Elias on the bench. Their shoulders brushed. The moment felt suspended the air thick with something sacred. Outside, the city moved restlessly beyond the high arched windows, the lights flickering like constellations brought down to earth.

Elias placed his hands on the keys first, pressing down softly a gentle ripple that echoed across the room.

The melody began, haunting and familiar, the same first bars of Eleanor's Waltz that had once changed the course of two lives.

Then Annabell joined him.

Her touch was light, tentative at first, like the cautious first steps of a dancer rejoining a partner after years apart. The harmony swelled between them, building, folding over itself. The music filled the room tender, graceful, mournful and yet there was something new within it.

Something alive.

Elias leaned into the rhythm, his fingers finding the progression Henry had written decades before. It was precise, beautiful, controlled. But then came the point where the sheet music ended where Henry had stopped, leaving behind a phrase unfinished, unresolved.

Annabell froze for just a moment, staring at the blank space on the page. Her heart pounded.

This was it the place where history had paused.

Elias looked at her, eyes filled with quiet encouragement.

And then, with trembling breath, Annabell began to play.

The melody she created was softer than the original more fragile, more human. It carried both grief and hope, rising and falling like a heartbeat that refused to give up. Her hands moved instinctively, guided not by thought, but by memory, by emotion, by something she couldn't explain.

Elias followed her, his harmony weaving beneath her melody like a promise kept through time. Together, their music became something larger than either of them a conversation between souls, old and new, between what had been lost and what had been found.

It was no longer Eleanor's Waltz.

It was Eleanor's Waltz II — For the Future.

The notes filled the ballroom with a brilliance that made the chandeliers tremble with reflected light. It was music that spoke of second chances, of courage, of love that refuses to die. And in the swell of its final crescendo, the air seemed to shimmer as though time itself had bent to listen.

Annabell's chest tightened as tears welled in her eyes. In the music, she could feel them — Eleanor and Henry not as ghosts, but as something more enduring. She could sense her Nana's warmth, her laughter, her forgiveness. She could almost see Henry's steady smile at the edge of the stage.

When the last note faded, silence fell heavy, luminous, infinite.

Annabell's hands hovered above the keys, trembling. Her breath came in shallow bursts as she looked at Elias. He was staring back at her, his expression unreadable, his eyes glistening.

Finally, he spoke. "You found the ending."

Annabell shook her head slowly, a tear slipping free. "No," she whispered. "They did."

For a moment, they just sat there, bathed in the golden hush of the ballroom. Outside, the rain had stopped. Through the windows, the city lights shimmered against the dark sky like scattered jewels. Somewhere far below, a taxi horns echoed faint and fleeting and the world began to move again.

But for Annabell and Elias, time stood still.

He reached over, his hand covering hers on the piano. "You know," he said softly, "that's the thing about love stories like theirs. They don't really end. They just... find new storytellers."

Annabell's lips curved into a faint smile, her heart swelling in her chest. "Maybe we're theirs now," she said quietly.

"Maybe we are," Elias murmured.

They sat like that for a long time two people surrounded by silence that wasn't empty, but full. Full of echoes, of music, of meaning. The hotel lights dimmed slightly as the night deepened, the chandeliers casting long shadows across the floor where once, long ago, Eleanor and Henry had danced.

Annabell looked out across that same polished marble now, her eyes reflecting the faint gleam of memory.

She could almost see them her Nana in her blue dress, Henry in his dark suit moving together in slow, perfect harmony. And in that vision, she saw something else too: herself, hand in hand with Elias, carrying the music forward.

When they finally rose from the bench, the room seemed to sigh as though exhaling after holding its breath for a century.

Elias turned to her, smiling softly. "You know," he said, "we should record it. The new waltz. Their story completed by you."

Annabell laughed gently, her heart warm. "Our story, maybe," she corrected.

"Maybe both," he replied.

They stood together at the edge of the stage, the city lights glimmering beyond the tall arched windows. The scent of lilies lingered faintly in the air, and from somewhere unseen, the sound of a violin drifted through the corridors soft, wistful, as though the Waldorf itself was humming approval.

Annabell turned her face upward toward the ceiling, her eyes shimmering. "Do you think she can hear it?"

Elias followed her gaze. "If music really does travel through time," he said quietly, "then she's dancing to it right now."

Annabell smiled, feeling her chest tighten with both joy and longing, "Then let's keep playing."

He nodded. "Always."

They returned to the piano not to end, but to begin again. The melody rose once more, filling the ballroom with light, with love, with the unbroken sound of forever.

And as the music carried them into the night, Annabell knew, truly knew that Eleanor's Waltz had been reborn.

It had found its new heartbeat.

Chapter 11

That next morning, sunlight seeped through the tall windows of the suite in slow ribbons. It touched the pale curtains, the soft cream of the duvet, the old mahogany dresser that had belonged to Eleanor Thorpe. The room still smelled faintly of lilies; Annabell had bought a small bouquet the day she arrived, setting it by the window as her grandmother had once done.

She was packing a few things for the studio when the drawer of the dresser stuck. She tugged again, harder, and it slid open with a sigh. Inside lay a jewellery box she had always known Nana's. A small oval case of polished walnut, its hinges dulled with age. She had kept it because it carried the scent of Eleanor's perfume and the faint clink of the pearls her grandmother had worn at her wedding.

On impulse, she lifted the lid. The familiar glint of brooches and delicate chains greeted her, but as she ran her fingers over the silk lining, she felt something rough beneath. A small corner of folded paper, wedged under the tray. It was so thin she might have missed it forever.

She hesitated, her heart quickening, then eased it free. The paper was yellowed and fragile, folded four times over. Her breath caught when she saw the handwriting. It was Henry's.

My dearest Eleanor,

If you ever find this, it means I was not brave enough to hand it to you when I should have. After you left, I wrote to you every day for weeks but never posted a single letter. Music was the only way I knew to speak without causing pain.

You once asked me why I called it "Eleanor's Waltz" and not simply "The Waltz." It is because you were never just a note in the song you were the rhythm itself. Without you, the melody could not stand.

There is a second piece unfinished, hidden among my sketches. It is yours to complete when your heart is ready. I could not finish it because it did not belong to me alone. It belongs to the one who carries your spirit forward.

If she should ever find it, tell her not to play it the way I did. Tell her to play it the way the world sounds when it begins again.

Yours, always,

Henry

Annabell's hands trembled as she read. The words blurred and steadied again as tears gathered at the corners of her eyes. She looked around the quiet room, the morning light spilling over the jewellery box, the pearls, the folded letter that had waited decades to be found.

Her voice broke into the silence. "You meant it for me, didn't you?"

She pressed the letter to her chest. The weight of it was small, but it filled her completely a connection, a permission, a blessing.

When she told Elias about the discovery later that morning, he listened without interrupting, his expression soft. They stood together in the recording studio the hotel had lent them, the same grand piano gleaming under warm lights. Microphones stood ready, the engineer waiting behind the glass.

Annabell placed the letter on the piano's lid. "He said the second waltz wasn't finished," she whispered. "He was waiting for her... and for whoever came after."

Elias nodded. "Then let's finish it properly. Let's make sure the world hears it."

As the first red light blinked on, the room fell into reverent quiet. Annabell took her seat beside him. She inhaled, steadying herself, and began to play.

The opening bars were the same the memory of Henry and Eleanor woven in sound. But then, guided by the words in that letter, the music shifted. Annabell added new phrases, airy and bright, like sunlight spilling through rain. Elias's chords met hers halfway, deep and warm.

The waltz no longer sounded like longing; it sounded like arrival.

Through the glass, the engineer sat motionless, moved beyond words. The last notes lingered until even the air seemed to shimmer. When they stopped, neither spoke for a long time.

Elias finally broke the silence. "He was right," he said quietly. "It does sound like the world beginning again."

Annabell traced the edge of the piano lid, her fingers resting beside the folded letter. "It feels like she's here. Both of them."

Outside, New York hummed, car horns, distant laughter, the endless rhythm of the city. Inside the studio, the new waltz settled into stillness, a living bridge between past and present.

Annabell turned to Elias, her eyes luminous. "Let's call it Eleanor's Waltz II: The Beginning."

He smiled. "Perfect."

The engineer's voice came through the speaker, hushed. "You want to run it again?"

Annabell looked down at Henry's handwriting, at the lines that had waited for her to read them. "Yes," she said softly. "Once more. For them."

Elias pressed record. The red light blinked. The piano keys glowed under the amber lamps. Their hands met over the keyboard, and the music rose again stronger, clearer, full of the life it had always sought.

Annabell felt it inside her chest, the pulse of generations: Henry's hope, Eleanor's courage, her own heart answering theirs. As the melody climbed, she knew this wasn't the end of their story.

It was only the next verse, the waltz still turning, the song still finding its way through time.

Chapter 12

When the record finally released, the world seemed to stop and listen.

It was a quiet Thursday morning in late May when Eleanor's Waltz II: The Beginning appeared on the streaming platforms and classical radio stations across London, New York, and Paris. There was no elaborate campaign, no fanfare just a simple cover: a sepia photograph of a grand piano in the Waldorf Astoria ballroom, with a single white lily resting on the lid.

The first few notes played softly through the radio in Annabell's flat. She stood by the window, coffee cooling in her hand, as the melody filled the small space her melody. Or rather, their melody. Hers, Elias's, Nana's, and Henry's.

The music floated around her like memory reborn. The strings entered halfway through a delicate orchestral arrangement that Elias had surprised her with during the final mix and it sounded as though the entire world had taken a breath. The piano still led the way, but now there was movement behind it: violins, cellos, woodwinds, a soft crescendo that felt like morning breaking through fog.

She closed her eyes and listened, her chest tightening. It was perfect imperfectly perfect, just as life had always been.

Elias arrived an hour later, rain clinging to his coat and the scent of the city on his clothes. He had a paper tucked under his arm — The New York Times, folded to the review section.

He handed it to her with a small, hesitant smile. "They heard it."

Annabell unfolded the page. Her breath caught at the headline.

A Love That Defied Time: "Eleanor's Waltz II" Is the Sound of Forever.

Her eyes skimmed the words —

"The piece carries the weight of two souls reunited through music, and yet there's something new in it hope, youth, a rebirth. The recording by Annabell Thorpe and Elias Moreau is not a continuation of Henry Dalton's legacy. It is its fulfilment."

Her throat constricted. She pressed the page to her chest. "Nana would have loved this," she whispered.

Elias smiled, though his eyes softened with emotion. "I think she's the one who made it happen."

Annabell turned toward him, a quiet laugh escaping through her tears. "Sometimes I think so too. The way things have unfolded how I found that letter when I did, how we met it feels too... orchestrated to be chance."

He tilted his head, watching her. "You think your grandmother and Henry arranged it from wherever they are?"

She met his gaze, a faint smile tugging at her lips. "Maybe they just nudged the rhythm a little. Maybe they knew the song wasn't finished not until it found its next players."

Elias's expression softened. He stepped closer, his hand brushing against hers. "And maybe it found them."

A silence fell between them, thick with unspoken things. For months they had worked side by side composing, recording, editing their lives folding together in small, delicate ways. Late nights at the studio. Shared glances that lingered longer than intended. Quiet laughter over coffee when words seemed too heavy.

Now, standing in her small London flat, the music they had created drifting faintly in the background, Annabell felt something deeper stir.

She looked at him really looked and for a heartbeat, she saw Henry again in his eyes. Not in appearance, but in spirit. The gentleness. The quiet strength. The love of music that came not from ambition, but from devotion.

Elias broke the silence first, his voice low. "Does it scare you?"

Annabell blinked. "What?"

"Feeling this," he said softly. "What's happening between us."

She hesitated. The truth was it did. Love had always felt to her like standing at the edge of something vast beautiful, but dangerous. She thought of her Nana at sixteen, standing in that same ballroom, torn between duty and desire. The fear of losing herself the way Eleanor once had.

But then she remembered how Eleanor had looked in those final years free, radiant, whole again because she'd finally chosen to follow her heart.

Annabell swallowed. "It scares me because it feels real. And real things... change you."

Elias reached out, brushing his thumb along her wrist, a touch so gentle it nearly broke her composure. "Maybe that's what loves meant to do."

For a long moment, neither of them moved. The rain tapped lightly against the glass, the city murmured beyond, and their music their waltz played softly between them, the piano rising and falling like breath.

Annabell felt her fear loosen, slowly, like a knot unravelling. She thought again of the letter Henry had written — "Tell her not to play it the way I did. Tell her to play it the way the world sounds when it begins again."

Maybe this was the world beginning again.

She looked up at Elias, her voice barely above a whisper. "Do you think... Nana wanted this for me? For us?"

Elias smiled, a hint of wonder in his eyes. "I think she and Henry started the music. We're just carrying it forward."

He drew her into his arms then not sudden, not rushed, but inevitable. She melted into him, her head resting against his shoulder as the final notes of Eleanor's Waltz II faded into silence.

In that stillness, Annabell felt something she hadn't in years, not just love but belonging. A sense of continuation. The unshakable feeling that her grandmother was there with them, smiling somewhere beyond the veil of time.

Later that night, when Elias had gone and the city had grown quiet, Annabell sat again by the window. The letter from Henry lay open on the table beside her, its edges worn, its words etched now into her heart.

She thought of the invisible hands that had guided her hearing her Nana's laughter, Henry's music, the shared courage of two souls who had loved fearlessly once and loved beyond the years that followed.

As the moon climbed higher, she whispered into the stillness, "You two planned this, didn't you?"

A gentle breeze slipped through the open window, brushing her cheek. The faint scent of lilies drifted in familiar, comforting.

She smiled, her eyes glistening. "Thank you."

And then, as if in answer, a faint echo of piano music rose from somewhere far below a waltz, soft and steady, threading through the night air. The same melody. The same rhythm. The same heartbeat.

Eleanor's and Henry's. Now hers and Elias's.

The legacy continued not as memory, but as living sound.

And as Annabell leaned back, listening, she felt something settle inside her: peace, hope, and a quiet certainty that love once true never fades. It simply changes players.

Chapter 13

The invitations came faster than either of them could have imagined.

Within weeks of its release, Eleanor's Waltz II: The Beginning had become an international phenom-enon. Classical radio stations played it daily; orches-tras requested the sheet music; dance companies began choreographing performances inspired by its rhythm. Critics called it "a piece that bridges generations — where love becomes melody and memory becomes sound."

But it wasn't the praise that moved Annabell the most it was the letters. Hundreds of them. Messages from people all over the world, widows, musicians, dreamers telling her that the waltz had touched them in ways they couldn't explain.

"My late husband and I danced to the original Eleanor's Waltz at our wedding," one letter read. "Hearing your version brought him back to me for three minutes. Thank you."

Each word deepened her conviction that the music had never truly belonged to one couple it belonged to everyone who had ever loved, lost, and hoped again.

And then came the invitation that made her heart stop.

It arrived embossed in gold and cream, signed by the Waldorf Astoria's director himself:

"We invite you and Mr. Elias Moreau to perform Eleanor's Waltz II: The Beginning live in the Grand Ballroom — the very place where Henry Dalton first played the original waltz. It will mark the 80th anniversary of his first performance."

Annabell sat at her piano with the letter trembling in her hands. For a moment, she couldn't breathe. The idea of returning to that ballroom of standing where Eleanor and Henry once stood felt both fated and terrifying.

She whispered to herself, "It's come full circle, Nana."

The night of the performance arrived like the opening of a story that had waited decades to be told.

New York was alive, the skyline glittering like a sea of diamonds under a velvet sky.

Outside the Waldorf, the street swelled with press and guests in formal attire, their excitement palpable in the cool spring air. The hotel's façade glowed in soft gold light, its windows gleaming like memories resurrected.

Inside, the Grand Ballroom had been transformed. The chandeliers blazed with light, scattering stars across the marble floor. Rows of velvet chairs faced the grand stage, where Henry's piano newly restored waited beneath a single spotlight. White lilies lined the edges of the stage, their scent delicate and nostalgic.

Every corner of the room seemed to hum with the presence of the past the very air alive with echoes of laughter and forgotten music.

Annabell stood backstage, her pulse racing. She wore a floor-length gown of midnight blue satin the same shade her Nana had once worn on the night she first met Henry. Around her neck hung Eleanor's pearl pendant, its lustre soft under the light.

Elias stood beside her, adjusting his cuffs, trying to mask his own nerves. He looked at her, his voice low but steady, "Are you ready, Annabell?"

She exhaled slowly. "I've never been ready for anything this much and never been this terrified either."

He smiled gently. "Then we're exactly where we're supposed to be."

She looked up at him, and for a fleeting second, the world fell away the crowd, the noise, the weight of expectation. All that remained was the quiet bond between them two hearts that had been drawn together by the same melody that once united two others.

When the stage manager signaled, Elias offered his hand. "Let's go make them feel what we feel."

Annabell took it. "For them," she whispered. "For Nana and Henry."

As they stepped into the light, a hush rippled through the ballroom. Cameras flashed, whispers stilled. Annabell could feel the weight of hundreds of eyes and yet, strangely, it didn't feel like pressure. It felt like presence. Like she wasn't alone.

She could almost sense her Nana's hand on her shoulder, the faint scent of rosewater lingering in the air.

Elias began first. The opening chords floated into the silence, soft and tender, like the sound of a heartbeat beginning anew. Annabell joined, her hands trembling only slightly before finding their rhythm. Together, their music blossomed into something luminous.

The crowd disappeared.

All that existed was the song the melody that carried the laughter of the past, the ache of lost years, and the soaring beauty of reunion.

As the strings from the accompanying orchestra rose, Annabell's emotions swelled with them. She could see it in her mind's eye Eleanor and Henry, dancing just beyond the veil of time, smiling as they spun beneath these same chandeliers.

Her eyes glistened as her fingers glided across the keys. Elias's harmony met hers perfectly, each note echoing his steadiness, his quiet admiration. Their connection pulsed through the music unspoken but undeniable.

By the time the piece reached its crescendo, the air in the ballroom felt electric. Every sound, every breath seemed to vibrate with energy the legacy of two love stories merging into one.

Annabell could feel tears slipping down her cheeks, but she didn't stop. She let them fall, let them mix with the music, because they belonged, their tears of gratitude, of wonder, of understanding.

When the final chord lingered long, aching, infinite the entire ballroom remained silent.

No one dared move, even the chandeliers seemed to still.

And then, slowly, the applause began soft at first, like the breaking of dawn, then swelling into thunderous ovation. People stood, clapping, cheering, some openly weeping.

Annabell looked up from the piano, breathless, heart racing. Elias reached for her hand, squeezing gently, "They're not just clapping for us," he said softly. "They're clapping for them."

She nodded, unable to speak. Her chest ached with emotion, with joy so full it was almost painful.

As they stood together on that stage, surrounded by applause, Annabell lifted her gaze to the balcony above. For a heartbeat, she saw them or thought she did. Eleanor and Henry, standing side by side in the soft glow of the chandeliers. Eleanor's silver hair gleamed, Henry's smile tender as ever.

They looked down at her, proud. Just like that, they were gone fading back into the light that seemed to fill every corner of the room.

Annabell blinked away her tears and turned back to Elias, "They're here," she whispered.

He smiled, the kind of smile that knew without needing proof, "I know."

Later that night, long after the audience had gone, Annabell and Elias remained in the ballroom. The chandeliers were dimmed now, and the only sound was the faint hum of the city outside.

Elias sat at the piano, playing softly, aimlessly improvising fragments of melody. Annabell leaned against the edge of the stage, watching him. Her heart was full and trembling all at once.

"They'd be proud of us," she said quietly.

"They are," Elias murmured. "You could feel it."

She smiled faintly. "It's strange, isn't it? How something written in heartbreak became something that brought so much love back into the world."

He glanced up at her, his expression tender. "Maybe that's what love always does it survives by changing shape."

Annabell's throat tightened. She walked toward him, her voice soft. "Elias... tonight felt like fate. Like everything every note, every choice, every heartbreak led here."

He looked up at her, his hand still resting on the keys. "It did."

Their eyes held for a long, breathless moment. Then, slowly, Elias rose from the bench and took her hand. The music stilled.

He drew her close, and in the dim glow of the chandeliers, they began to sway no orchestra, no audience, just the faint hum of the city and the lingering heartbeat of Eleanor's Waltz II.

Annabell rested her head against his chest. She could hear his heartbeat, steady and warm.

And in that moment, surrounded by history, love, and memory, she felt utterly, beautifully alive.

The past had given them its blessing. Now, the future was theirs to write.

Chapter 14

The days that followed their Waldorf performance blurred into a golden haze.

Everywhere they went, people spoke of Eleanor's Waltz II: The Beginning not as a revival of an old classic, but as something living. Newspapers called it "a miracle of music and memory." A London critic wrote, "The Thorpe legacy has returned to remind the world that love, once found, is never lost only transposed."

Annabell read the articles in the quiet mornings she and Elias shared in cafés tucked along New York's streets. The city felt different now: brighter, more forgiving, as if the music had softened even its edges. Yet fame, for her, didn't feel like triumph. It felt like purpose.

At night, she and Elias returned to the Waldorf's piano. They would play together long after the staff had gone home just two figures beneath the chande-liers, their reflections moving across the polished floor. Sometimes they spoke little; the music said what words could not.

And somewhere between the melodies and silences, their connection deepened.

Elias had a way of watching her when she played not out of admiration but understanding. She could feel him listening to her heart rather than her notes. In those moments, Annabell began to realize that love, for her, was no longer something she waited to find. It was something she had quietly grown into.

Summer — Paris

The tour began in July. Their first performance outside New York was in Paris, at the Théâtre des Champs-Élysées a city Henry Dalton had once dreamed of playing but never reached.

As they stepped onto that grand stage, the lights caught the curve of the piano, making it shimmer like glass. Annabell wore a flowing gown the colour of champagne, Elias, his black suit and steady composure. The orchestra behind them waited, poised.

Before they began, Annabell spoke to the audience.

"My grandmother, Eleanor Thorpe, once said that music remembers what the heart cannot forget. Tonight, we play for those who have loved and for those still waiting to."

The room was utterly still. Then, they began.

The waltz rippled through the air familiar, yet fresh. It no longer belonged only to the past. In Paris, it found new meaning: the laughter of strangers, the quiet tears of listeners who didn't know the story but somehow felt it. When the final chord echoed, the crowd rose to their feet, clapping until Annabell felt tears break free.

Afterward, in the dressing room, Elias touched her cheek gently, "You did it," he said.

"No," she whispered, "we did."

Autumn — Vienna, Tokyo, Rome

They travelled from city to city, the world opening before them like a sheet of music waiting to be played. Vienna, where audiences wept openly. Tokyo, where the precision of the orchestra made the waltz sound almost ethereal. Rome, where candlelight from the opera house flickered over the stage, and the audience threw lilies instead of roses.

In each city, Annabell felt her grandmother near sometimes in a dream, sometimes in the sudden scent of rosewater, or the faint impression of a whisper just before she played. It no longer frightened her. It comforted her.

At night, when the crowds were gone, she would lie awake beside Elias in quiet hotel rooms across continents. He would trace idle circles on her wrist and talk softly about their next stop, their next stage. Sometimes they said nothing at all, content just to exist in the fragile space where legacy and love met.

But there were moments when Annabell felt something deeper stirring a question she hadn't yet dared to ask aloud: What comes after?

Her life had become entwined with a story that began long before she was born. She had spent years carrying it forward, shaping it, honouring it. But now, as her own name began to appear beside Eleanor's and Henry's in concert programs and interviews, she began to sense that perhaps her grandmother's dream hadn't ended with the waltz it was unfolding still, through her.

Winter — Return to London

By December, Eleanor's Waltz II had reached the top of the classical charts worldwide. Invitations arrived daily. But Annabell wanted one more concert a small one in London, the city where she had first played alone, where she had composed Legacy in the stillness of grief.

The night of the performance, the theatre glowed with golden light, frost shimmering on the windows outside. The audience was intimate friends, fellow musicians, people who had followed their story from the beginning.

Elias waited with her backstage, his hand brushing hers as he leaned closer.

"Do you still feel them?" he asked quietly.

Annabell smiled faintly, looking toward the stage. "Every night. But it's changing."

"How?" "It's like they're farther away now but not gone. Like they're making space for me to write my own story."

He studied her face, his eyes soft. "Then maybe that's what destiny is not repeating theirs but continuing it."

She turned toward him, heart swelling. "Elias... what if this was what Nana wanted all along? Not for me to follow her path, but to finish it to live freely, love fearlessly, create without fear of loss."

He smiled, his hand cupping her cheek. "Then you've done exactly that."

Their lips met softly the kind of kiss that felt less like a beginning and more like recognition. It wasn't a promise made; it was one already kept.

After the Concert

When they finished playing that night, the applause felt different. Not thunderous gentle, sincere, the sound of understanding. As Annabell bowed, she looked out at the audience and saw people holding hands, leaning on one another, smiling through tears. She realized, then, that the waltz had become something far greater than her family's story.

It had become everyone's.

Backstage, the theatre manager approached with an envelope, "A delivery came for you, Miss Thorpe. No sender."

Inside, on cream stationery, written in the looping cursive she knew by heart, were just two words:

Keep dancing.

Annabell's breath caught. The paper smelled faintly of lilies.

Elias stepped behind her, resting a hand on her shoulder, "What is it?"

She turned, smiling through tears. "A message from them."

He didn't ask how she knew. He just nodded, the corners of his mouth curving upward.

They stood in the quiet corridor, the muffled sounds of the audience still lingering beyond the walls. Annabell felt the warmth of his hand, the letter pressed to her heart, and for the first time, she wasn't afraid of what came next.

Because she finally understood: Eleanor and Henry's love hadn't ended. It had simply changed hands passed from one generation to the next, from piano to piano, from heart to heart.

Now, it was her turn to play.

The curtain hadn't fallen; it had merely lifted again.

Annabell Thorpe was no longer just the granddaughter of Eleanor. She was her own composer, her own storyteller, and the world listening now, waiting was her stage.

Chapter 15

Two months later, winter had loosened its grip on New York. The city shimmered in that early-spring haze where the air still bit but the sunlight hinted at warmth. Outside the Waldorf Astoria, the streets glowed with puddled reflections, taxis sliding by in slow rhythm.

Annabell Thorpe stood on the curb, her scarf wound tight against the wind, gazing up at the hotel's familiar façade. Every visit here felt like stepping into another century, another heartbeat. Yet today was different. Today, she was not returning to play Eleanor's Waltz or to echo the past. She was here to begin something new.

Inside, the lobby still smelled faintly of lilies and polished oak. The golden light along the staircase bathed the marble in warmth. Guests drifted by, unaware that history breathed quietly in the corners. Annabell brushed her fingertips over the banister as she climbed, half expecting to hear her grandmother's laughter on the landing.

Elias was already in the ballroom when she arrived. The chandeliers were dimmed, leaving only soft pools of light around the grand piano. Sheet music lay scattered across the lid pages filled with her handwriting. The title at the top read: "The Passage of Time."

He looked up from the bench and smiled. "It feels right, doesn't it?"

She nodded, setting her bag down. "It's the only name that ever fit. It's about them, but also about us. About how everything moves forward, even when it circles back."

Elias leaned back slightly, watching her as she traced the piano's edge. "What made you start writing again?"

Annabell thought for a moment. "I woke up one night in London, hearing music in my head. It wasn't Eleanor's Waltz it was something lighter, like dawn after a long night. I realized it wasn't about remembrance anymore. It was about continuation."

He gestured toward the piano. "Play it for me."

She hesitated, heart fluttering. "It's not finished."

He smiled. "Neither was the last one."

Annabell sat beside him, her fingers trembling over the keys. When she began to play, the sound was soft a gentle, rippling motif that felt like time breathing. It carried echoes of Eleanor's Waltz, yes, but it was warmer, more fluid, like sunlight through glass. The melody wove between minor and major, rising then resolving with quiet grace.

Elias joined in, adding low chords that grounded the piece, giving it weight. Their music filled the ballroom again not nostalgic, not haunted, but alive. It spoke of motion, of legacy transforming.

Annabell closed her eyes, letting her thoughts drift. She saw Eleanor and Henry in flashes laughing beneath chandeliers, writing notes on napkins, holding hands in secret gardens. She saw herself and Elias airports, concert halls, quiet mornings over coffee, laughter spilling between rehearsals. The two stories blurred until they became one.

When the final note faded, Annabell's hands rested still on the keys. She felt tears prick behind her eyes not of sadness, but of awe.

Elias turned to her. "It's beautiful," he said softly. "It feels like forgiveness and beginning all at once."

She smiled through the shimmer in her vision. "That's what I wanted. To show that love doesn't just echo it evolves. It grows with every generation that dares to remember."

He reached over, brushing a strand of hair from her face. "Then this is your legacy now. Not just Eleanor's Waltz, but everything that came after."

Annabell leaned into his touch, her heart steady. "Ours," she whispered. "It's ours now."

That evening, they recorded the first version of The Passage of Time. No orchestra, no audience just the two of them and the hush of the Waldorf ballroom. The microphones caught every breath, every faint vibration of the strings. Outside, the city lights blinked like distant stars reflected on wet pavement.

As they played, the tempo shifted subtly faster, lighter, almost like a heartbeat finding its pace again.

It was not a farewell; it was an awakening. The song felt like stepping through a doorway into morning.

When they finished, silence lingered before Elias spoke, "She would be proud, you know."

Annabell smiled faintly. "I think she's here. I can almost feel her."

He looked around the room, his voice low. "It's strange. I used to think music died when people did. But maybe it's the opposite. Maybe it's what keeps them alive."

Annabell placed her hand over his. "Music is the memory the world refuses to forget."

They sat together in the dim light, the echoes of their song still trembling through the floor. Annabell's gaze drifted upward to the crystal chandeliers each reflection like a star waiting to fall. She thought of everything that had led here: her grandmother's courage, Henry's devotion, the letter hidden in the jewellery box, the endless journey of love through time.

For the first time, she felt no divide between then and now. Just one continuous melody the passage of time, ever turning, ever renewing.

When they left the ballroom, dawn was breaking over the city. The streets were washed in pale gold, and the first warmth of the sun spilled across the stone steps of the Waldorf. Annabell paused at the door, looking back once more.

The piano stood alone under the fading light, silent but alive, as if it waited for its next song.

Elias reached for her hand. "Where to next?"

Annabell smiled, eyes bright. "Wherever the music takes us."

As they stepped into the morning, she whispered a quiet promise to the world that had given her so much, "For you, Nana. For Henry. For every love that endures."

The city answered with its endless hum, and somewhere deep within it, she thought she heard faint notes of a waltz timeless, tender, and forever beginning again.

Chapter 16

The night of the premiere arrived wrapped in velvet and light.

Winter had given way to spring, and New York gleamed beneath a silver sky. At Lincoln Center, the plaza's fountain glimmered like liquid glass, its arcs of water catching the golden reflections of the chandeliers beyond the grand lobby. Crowds gathered beneath the wide marble steps critics, musicians, admirers all drawn by the promise of a single performance: The Passage of Time, the newest work by Annabell Thorpe and Elias Moreau.

It wasn't just another concert. It was a moment years in the making a continuation of a love story that had lived across generations, through notes and echoes, through the unbroken rhythm of a waltz that refused to fade.

Annabell stood backstage, heart racing beneath her silver gown. The fabric shimmered with every breath, catching the soft glow of the sconces. She smoothed her palms against the satin, trying to steady herself. Her reflection in the mirror stared back poised, elegant but inside, she was a storm of anticipation.

She looked toward the piano waiting under the lights. The orchestra tuned quietly behind the curtain, strings humming softly like a heartbeat in the dark. She could smell the faint sweetness of lilies a scent she hadn't requested, but one that seemed to follow her wherever she performed.

Nana's scent.

Annabell pressed a hand to her chest. "You're here," she whispered.

A gentle voice came from behind, "You ready?"

Elias stood in the doorway, dressed in a tailored black suit, his tie slightly loose as always, his eyes calm yet shining. His presence had become her anchor the stillness before the first note.

"Ready?" she repeated with a nervous laugh. "I've been dreaming about this moment for months. And now that it's here, I feel like I might forget how to breathe."

He smiled softly. "Then I'll breathe for you until you remember."

That simple line melted the air between them. Annabell reached for his hand, fingers trembling. "What if it doesn't live up to what people expect? To what she would expect?"

Elias shook his head, eyes steady on hers. "It already does. This isn't just her story anymore it's yours. You finished what she began. That's all she ever wanted."

The stage manager's voice broke through the curtain. "Two minutes!"

Annabell inhaled deeply. "Alright," she whispered. "Let's give them time itself."

When the curtain lifted, a hush swept across the hall.

The stage gleamed beneath soft amber light. Behind her, the orchestra sat ready, violins poised, cellos humming in anticipation. Elias stood to her left, hands folded, his calm presence grounding her.

The applause faded. Annabell took her place at the piano.

The first note she played was fragile, hesitant like dawn touching the horizon. Then came another, then another the melody unfolding in slow, graceful arcs. The orchestra followed, the strings swelling like wind through open fields. The rhythm carried both melancholy and hope the sound of time turning, of moments slipping and returning in endless circles.

As she played, images rose in her mind: her Nana dancing under chandeliers, Henry's hands gliding over the keys, Elias watching her across hotel lobbies and rehearsal rooms. The past and present merged until she couldn't tell where one ended and the other began.

The waltz theme returned briefly faint, almost like a whisper before dissolving into something entirely new. A rising, symphonic passage that felt like breath expanding, like the heart rediscovering its rhythm.

She could feel the audience breathing with her every soul in the room tethered to the same invisible thread.

Elias's harmony joined hers, their music weaving in and out of each other like conversation. It was intimate and vast all at once two lives speaking across a stage, their story told through sound.

The crescendo came, it was not thunderous but luminous a surge of light breaking through shadow. The violins soared, the piano echoed upward, and for a moment, Annabell felt something beyond words: Her grandmother's laughter, Henry's devotion, her own heart opening to the infinite.

When the final note faded, silence filled the hall the kind of silence that feels alive, humming with everything unsaid.

Then, applause erupted. Thunderous. Endless. A standing ovation that rolled through the room like a wave.

Annabell looked up, tears shining in her eyes. She turned to Elias, and he smiled not the polite smile of a performer, but the quiet, full smile of someone who understood what the moment meant.

They bowed together, and the lights above caught the glint of the pearl pendant resting against Annabell's throat Eleanor's.

Somewhere deep within, she felt it: pride, peace, and a gentle warmth that felt like an embrace from the past.

Later that night, after the hall emptied, they returned to the stage. The chandeliers had dimmed, leaving only the soft amber glow of the exit lights. The fountain outside murmured faintly through the glass. Annabell sat on the piano bench again, tracing the edge of the keys.

"It's strange," she murmured. "The more I play, the closer I feel to them but also, the farther away. Like they're stepping back, letting me stand on my own."

Elias sat beside her, his expression tender. "That's what they wanted. They carried the song as far as they could. You carried it farther. Maybe now it's time for you to write your own."

She glanced at him, heart swelling. "A symphony," she whispered.

His eyebrows lifted slightly. "A symphony?"

"Yes," she said, voice trembling with excitement. "For her for Eleanor. Not just a waltz, not just a memory. A full symphony about love through time. About how we never really lose the people we love we just learn to hear them differently."

Elias reached for her hand, his thumb tracing slow circles against her skin. "Then let's write it. Together."

Annabell's heart fluttered, that familiar mix of fear and wonder, "Together," she echoed, her voice barely a breath.

For a while, they sat in silence, listening to the city hum through the walls. Then Elias leaned closer, his voice low. "You know," he said, "I think your grandmother and Henry planned all of this every note, every coincidence, every breath that brought us here."

Annabell smiled, tears shimmering again, "Then they've written the most beautiful duet in history."

He laughed softly. "And left us to write the finale."

Outside, New York pulsed with light and life. Inside, the last echoes of The Passage of Time lingered in the air not as an ending, but as an opening.

Annabell leaned against Elias, feeling the slow rhythm of his heartbeat beside hers. For the first time, she didn't feel caught between eras. The past no longer weighed her down; it lifted her. The future no longer frightened her; it invited her.

She looked at the piano the instrument that had carried generations of love she whispered softly, "It's time."

Elias tilted his head. "For what?"

She smiled through quiet tears. "For our own song."

The lights dimmed fully then, leaving the stage bathed in silver from the moon beyond the windows.

The piano waited, silent but expectant as if it already knew that another melody, another story, was about to begin.

Somewhere in the hush, between the faint echoes of applause and the heartbeat of the city, Annabell could almost hear them Eleanor and Henry laughing softly, waltzing one last time as the music turned another page.

Chapter 17

Spring melted fully into summer, and the Waldorf's windows breathed in the hum of the city below. Annabell had rented a small apartment just three blocks away—a sun-washed loft that smelled faintly of varnish and rain. The wide windows overlooked the park; in the evenings the light spilled across the wooden floor like liquid gold. That room became their studio.

Most mornings began the same way: coffee cooling beside the piano, loose pages scattered like snow, and the faint sound of traffic rising and falling like a metronome. Elias would sit cross-legged on the rug with his violin across his knees, eyes closed, tracing invisible notes in the air. Annabell, perched on the bench, would test fragments on the keys—soft phrases, half-finished ideas that hovered between melody and memory.

She called it The Symphony for Eleanor, but in her heart, it already had another name: A Life Remembered.

The music came slowly at first, in threads rather than themes. Some days she felt as though the waltz still lingered too close, shadowing every bar. She wanted this new work to breathe differently—to begin where the waltz had ended, to move forward into light. But how do you write about a love that has already crossed time itself?

She would close her eyes and picture her grandmother at the piano in 1946, fingers trembling with first love, and then picture herself now different and yet the same, another heartbeat in the same measure. The thought both steadied and unsettled her. If she could see me now, would she understand what I'm trying to say?

Elias broke her reverie one morning. "You're holding back," he said gently.

Annabell looked up from the keys. "Maybe I'm afraid. The waltz was easy it already existed. This... this has to come from me."

He stood, came behind her, and placed his hands lightly on her shoulders. "Then let it. Don't write about them anymore. Write what they gave you."

Something inside her unlocked at that. That afternoon the first true movement took shape: a slow rising theme in D major, tender but confident, the sound of stepping into one's own life. Elias added a countermelody on violin, rich, human, a voice answering hers. The two lines met and parted like breath. When they stopped, the room seemed to glow.

She turned to him, eyes shining. "That's it. That's the beginning."

He smiled, the corners of his mouth soft. "Feels like morning after a long night."

Days passed in a blur of music and quiet conversation. They ate late dinners over manuscripts, sometimes arguing about tempo or phrasing, sometimes laughing until the candles burned out. The walls filled with sound sketches pinned in uneven rows—bits of melody that marked their progress like constellations.

Outside, New York sweltered; inside, time seemed suspended. The loft became a world of its own half sanctuary, half storm. On humid nights they would leave the windows open, letting the breeze stir the pages while the city's heartbeat pulsed through the curtains.

Annabell began to sense the shape of the symphony:

Movement I — "Awakening."

Movement II — "Memory and Light."

Movement III — "Legacy."

Movement IV — "The Passage."

Each movement felt like a lifetime, hers, Eleanor's, Henry's, all merging. She wrote the second one during a rainstorm, the drops drumming against the glass like a distant percussion. Elias sat beside her, his hand resting lightly on her back as she played through the fragile middle section. It was a lullaby to everything lost, and when she finished, tears streaked her cheeks.

He didn't speak; he simply reached for her hand and pressed his lips to her knuckles. The gesture said what words could not: I'm here. Keep going.

By late August the final movement was forming. It was unlike anything she'd ever written broad, luminous, filled with ascending harmonies that seemed to lift the listener off the ground. She called it The Passage because it felt like standing on the threshold between worlds. When she played it straight through for the first time, the air in the room seemed to hum.

Elias listened in silence, his bow resting on his lap. When the last chord faded, he whispered, "That's not just for her anymore. That's you."

Annabell leaned back, breathless. "I think it's all of us," she said. "Her, Henry... you."

He met her gaze, and the quiet between them deepened no longer just collaboration, but communion. The music had woven their souls together, thread by thread, until she could no longer tell where one melody ended and the other began.

That night they left the windows open and let the city's lights spill across the floor. Annabell sat cross-legged beside the piano, head resting on Elias's shoulder. The room smelled of ink, coffee, and rain. Outside, a siren wailed somewhere far off, fading into the hum of traffic. Inside, peace settled like a sigh.

"I used to think legacy meant preserving the past," she murmured. "But maybe it's about creating something that lets it keep moving."

Elias turned his head slightly, brushing his lips against her hair. "Then you've done it. The waltz was memory. The symphony is life."

Annabell closed her eyes, listening to the soft rhythm of his breathing, and realized that love, real love wasn't about finding a reflection of the past. It was about building harmony out of difference, about daring to keep composing even when the music changes key.

When morning came, the first sunlight spilled across the piano, turning the pages of the Symphony for Eleanor pale gold. The final measure waited still unfinished a single bar, empty, expectant. Annabell smiled, knowing she would leave it that way. Some stories, after all, are meant to keep playing.

Chapter 18

Autumn returned to New York like a soft exhale crisp air, golden trees bowing to the wind, the skyline painted in shades of copper and dusk. The Waldorf Astoria, reborn once again in all its timeless grace, stood at the heart of it all. Its grand lobby shimmered with chandeliers that had seen generations pass beneath their light, and tonight, they would witness something extraordinary the world premiere of The Symphony for Eleanor.

Outside, a line of guests stretched down the marble steps, critics, musicians, patrons, families, and lovers. The anticipation was palpable, electric. The story of Eleanor's Waltz had captured hearts across decades, but now, this was something greater something that belonged not just to history, but to eternity.

Annabell stood backstage in the grand ballroom, her hands trembling slightly as she adjusted the sleeve of her gown a soft ivory silk that caught the light like moon water. Around her neck glowed Eleanor's pearl pendant, and in her chest, her heart thudded with equal parts terror and wonder.

She looked toward the orchestra settling on stage a sea of black and white, bows poised, brass gleaming under the chandeliers. At the centre stood Elias, baton in hand, his presence steady and commanding. The sight of him, calm amid the storm, made her pulse slow, her breath deepen.

He turned, meeting her gaze across the stage. His lips curved in a small, knowing smile a quiet promise that they had already won, simply by reaching this moment.

Annabell exhaled, feeling the past and present fold gently into one another. Nana... we made it.

She could almost feel her grandmother's hand on her shoulder, that same familiar warmth that had always followed her before every performance. The scent of lilies drifted faintly from somewhere unseen, mingling with the faint resin of the violins and the wax of the polished floor.

The director's voice echoed softly over the microphone:

"Ladies and gentlemen, thank you for joining us tonight for the world premiere of The Symphony for Eleanor, composed by Annabell Thorpe, conducted by Elias Moreau a continuation of the legacy that began here nearly a century ago with Eleanor's Waltz."

Applause swelled rich, expectant.

Annabell took her seat at the piano, her hands hovering above the keys. The stage lights dimmed to gold. For a moment, the world seemed to hold its breath.

Elias raised his baton. The hall fell utterly still.

Then it began.

The first movement Awakening rose like dawn breaking. A single piano phrase shimmered, delicate as breath, before the strings joined, expanding it into warmth. The melody felt like opening a window after years of silence. Annabell's hands moved gently, her fingers dancing as though guided by unseen memory.

The sound filled the ballroom with light the kind of light that feels alive, golden, forgiving.

In the second movement Memory and Light the orchestra swelled, intertwining violins with the piano's soft echo. It was here that Annabell felt her throat tighten. This was Eleanor's voice not as longing, but as laughter, as grace remembered. She played through tears, her vision blurring, yet her hands never faltered.

The audience was transfixed. You could hear the faintest breaths, soft gasps as the music painted love in sound. It wasn't performance anymore. It was prayer.

The third movement Legacy changed everything. A shift in tempo. Brass entered bold and bright carrying Henry's spirit, the fearless energy of a man who had loved beyond the rules of his time. The piano responded not in sorrow, but in triumph, echoing him, answering him across years.

Annabell felt Elias's eyes on her as he conducted every motion a conversation between them, every rise of his baton another heartbeat shared. In those moments, she no longer felt separated by generations. She and

Elias weren't merely continuing a story; they were part of the same endless song.

When the fourth movement arrived The Passage, the lights dimmed even softer, and the world seemed to narrow to the space between one note and the next.

The music slowed. Time slowed.

A gentle waltz motif whispered through the strings a memory of the first Eleanor's Waltz, fragile and pure. Annabell closed her eyes as she played, letting her heart lead. She could see them Eleanor and Henry beneath the chandeliers of decades past, swaying slowly, smiling. The melody rose, transformed, no longer bound by sadness but lifted by joy.

Elias lowered his baton slightly and let the orchestra fade until only Annabell remained just the piano, echoing through the silent hall. She played the final passage with trembling hands, her soul laid bare in every note. The music swelled, brightened, and then silence.

The pause afterward stretched forever.

Then, the audience rose. The applause roared a tidal wave of sound. People shouted bravo! others wept openly. Critics, musicians, strangers all on their feet, clapping until the hall itself seemed to vibrate.

Annabell stood slowly, her heart pounding, her eyes glistening with tears. She turned toward Elias. He set down his baton, smiling softly, his gaze filled with emotion. He mouthed one word: Always.

She stepped forward, taking his hand, and together they bowed.

In that bow, the world seemed to fold into stillness two souls linked by something larger than fame, larger than music.

Later, after the applause faded and the lights dimmed, the ballroom emptied to a hush. Only the faint hum of the city lingered beyond the windows.

Annabell and Elias sat side by side on the stage, the orchestra gone, the piano still warm beneath her fingertips. She leaned her head against his shoulder, exhausted, elated, "I think we did it," she whispered.

He smiled. "You did more than that. You gave her eternity."

Annabell laughed softly, shaking her head. "No. She gave it to me."

They sat in silence for a long time, listening to the echo of the last note still hanging in the air faint, invisible, eternal. Through the tall windows, the moon cast silver light across the marble floor, and in it, Annabell could almost see the reflection of two other figures Eleanor and Henry, holding each other as they had once done, their faces soft with pride.

Tears pricked her eyes again, but this time they were tears of peace.

Elias reached for her hand, their fingers intertwining. "So," he said softly, "what comes after a symphony?"

Annabell smiled faintly, her heart full. "Life," she whispered. "Everything that comes after."

And as they sat beneath the chandeliers the past behind them, the future humming quietly ahead Annabell felt the truth settle deep within her:

Love doesn't end. It changes form ... from waltz to symphony, from echo to heartbeat, from memory to creation.

Outside, the city glowed. Inside, the last light from the chandeliers shimmered across the empty stage, catching the gold lettering on the program that lay open on the piano lid:

The Symphony for Eleanor

Composed by Annabell Thorpe

Conducted by Elias Moreau

"Time is but music waiting to be played."

As the final echoes of applause dissolved into the night, the music and their story continued, softly, endlessly, into forever.

Chapter 19

A month had passed since The Symphony for Eleanor had filled the Waldorf with its final, trembling chord, but its echoes still seemed to move through the city like an invisible tide. Every café that played classical music carried its opening theme. Every review spoke of how it had changed the air that night. And for Annabell Thorpe and Elias Moreau, the world had become quieter, gentler as though the music had burned away the noise and left only clarity behind.

They had not rushed to their next project. Instead, they slipped away.

Florence

The early autumn sun poured over the Arno, gilding the bridges and terracotta roofs. Annabell leaned against the balcony of their rented apartment, sketchbook in hand, watching the river move in lazy ribbons of light. Below, the city breathed vendors calling softly in Italian, bells from Santa Croce marking the hour.

Elias sat behind her, tuning his violin, the sound mingling with the distant laughter of street musicians. Their days here were slow, filled with music that asked for nothing in return.

Annabell wrote in her journal:

It's strange to live without an audience again. The quiet feels like a rest between movements necessary, but uncertain. I keep thinking about the moment the symphony ended, and how I wanted to start again immediately. But now... I think perhaps the next composition isn't written on paper. It's written in how we live.

She turned to Elias, smiling faintly. "Do you ever think about what comes next?"

He lowered his bow. "Every day. But not with fear anymore. Before you, I used to think music was the only way to prove I existed. Now it's just the way I breathe."

His honesty struck her simple, unguarded. She had learned, slowly, that silence between them carried more truth than a hundred spoken promises.

That night, they dined in a small trattoria near Piazza della Repubblica. The air was fragrant with basil and red wine. Candles flickered across white tablecloths. Annabell's laughter came easily freer now, lighter. When Elias reached across the table and took her hand, she didn't pull away. She only thought of how far they had come from a chance encounter in the Waldorf ballroom to this soft, golden evening, the world around them humming with possibility.

By winter, invitations began to arrive again orchestras, universities, museums. Everyone wanted them to speak about the waltz, the symphony, the legacy.

Annabell would spread the letters across the kitchen table, sipping tea while Elias read aloud in mock formality.

"'Professor Thorpe and Maestro Moreau are invited to host a masterclass on intergenerational composition at the Conservatoire in Paris...'" He grinned. "I think they're calling us old."

Annabell laughed, shaking her head. "I'm barely thirty-six."

"That's practically ancient in musician years," he teased.

They decided to accept a few not the grand ones, but the intimate ones, the schools where young musicians still scribbled notes by hand and played until their fingers blistered. They travelled lightly, teaching from memory and feeling rather than theory.

In one quiet class in Vienna, a student asked Annabell, "How do you write about something you've never lived?"

Annabell paused, glancing at Elias. "You don't," she said softly. "You listen to what's already inside you. It's all their love, loss, hope. You just have to be brave enough to play it."

Later that night, Elias told her, "You sound like her when you teach."

"Like whom?"

"Eleanor."

The name hung between them like music. Annabell smiled wistfully, "Maybe she's the one teaching through me."

Back in New York, snow pressed softly against the windows of their apartment. The city below was muted horns muffled, footsteps cushioned. Annabell sat at the piano with a blanket over her shoulders, sketching melodies on thin paper. Elias watched her from the couch, a cup of coffee cooling in his hands.

"What is it this time?" he asked.

"I don't know yet," she said. "It's something smaller just a whisper of a piece. Maybe for solo piano. Something to say thank you."

"To who?"

She smiled faintly. "To them. To time itself."

He stood, came behind her, and wrapped his arms around her shoulders. Together they listened to the silence outside the kind of silence that hums after snow, when the world feels newly written.

Annabell rested her head against his arm. "Do you ever wonder if we would've found each other without them?"

He thought for a long moment. "I don't think we were supposed to find each other without them. They were the overture. We're the rest of the score."

The thought made her chest ache with quiet joy. Theirs wasn't a love born of coincidence. It was inheritance not of wealth or name, but of music, of courage, of faith in beauty.

Months later, as spring crept back into the city, Annabell sat by the river, her notebook open on her knees. She wrote slowly, deliberately:

The waltz taught me memory.

The symphony taught me becoming.

Now, life teaches me the silence between the notes where love grows quietly, unannounced, but endless.

She looked up at the skyline the Waldorf visible in the distance, its windows glinting in the morning light. She could almost hear faint strains of Eleanor's Waltz in the wind, like a whisper from beyond the years.

Elias joined her, slipping an arm around her waist. "What are you thinking about?"

She smiled, closing the notebook. "About how everything that begins in music ends in love."

He kissed the top of her head. "Then we're still playing."

And they were.

Not in concert halls this time, but in the gentle rhythm of shared mornings, the laughter over burnt toast, the quiet nights when she played until dawn and he listened half-asleep, smiling.

The music hadn't ended. It had simply found a new home in their lives, in the space between their breaths, in every heartbeat that dared to keep time.

Outside, the city stirred awake. The sun rose higher, washing the river in gold. Annabell and Elias stood watching it, the air cool, their hands intertwined. Behind them lay generations of melody and memory. Ahead unplayed notes, unwritten movements.

Annabell whispered to the morning, "Let's see where the music goes next."

Elias squeezed her hand. "Together?"

"Always," she said.

The day opened before them, bright and endless another measure in the symphony of forever.

Chapter 20

The years slipped by like pages turning softly in a beloved book.

New York changed, as all cities do buildings rose higher, the skyline glimmered brighter, but the Waldorf Astoria remained like a steadfast heartbeat at its center: elegant, timeless, carrying its own quiet pulse of memory.

It was spring again though a gentler one when Annabell and Elias returned to its marble steps. The invitation had arrived months earlier:

The Waldorf Astoria invites you to the 100th Anniversary Celebration of "Eleanor's Waltz" — featuring a special performance of "The Symphony for Eleanor."

Annabell had stared at the letter for a long time that morning, her fingers tracing the embossed gold lettering. She was no longer the trembling woman she had once been on that stage, uncertain and searching. There were faint lines now at the corners of her eyes — not from sadness, but from laughter. Her hair had lightened with streaks of silver that caught the sun like threads of memory.

Elias stood beside her on the hotel steps, his hand warm around hers. Time had been kind to him, softening his edges without dimming the fire in his eyes. There was still that quiet steadiness in him, the calm that anchored her even when the music faltered.

He glanced up at the grand facade. "It looks exactly the same."

Annabell smiled, her heart swelling. "It feels the same, too."

Inside, the lobby glowed with familiar light. Chandeliers spilled golden reflections across the marble floor. Fresh lilies filled crystal vases, their perfume subtle but unmistakable the scent of remembrance. Guests milled about in elegant attire, murmuring with anticipation, unaware that for Annabell and Elias, this was not merely a concert. It was a homecoming.

They were ushered into the Grand Ballroom, and for a moment, Annabell froze at the threshold.

It was as though time had folded neatly upon itself. The same vaulted ceiling, the same chandeliers, the same hushed reverence before music begins. She could almost see shadows of the past layered over the present Henry at the piano, Eleanor in her blue dress, the young version of herself walking toward destiny without realizing it.

Elias squeezed her hand gently, "You, okay?"

Annabell nodded, her eyes glistening. "Yes. I just... it feels like they're all here again."

He smiled. "Maybe they never left."

The thought made her chest ache in that familiar, beautiful way the ache of something too vast to name.

When the orchestra began to tune, the hall quieted. The air seemed charged, almost sacred. The program listed Eleanor's Waltz first performed by a young pianist Annabell had once mentored, a prodigy named Clara.

As Clara stepped onto the stage, slender and radiant, Annabell felt pride swell in her chest. Watching her was like glimpsing her younger self wide-eyed, full of awe and hope.

The first notes of Eleanor's Waltz rang through the ballroom delicate, trembling, heartbreakingly familiar. The melody drifted through the air like smoke, curling around the chandeliers and settling deep into every soul present.

Annabell closed her eyes. She was transported instantly to the ballroom decades ago, her Nana and Henry finding one another after a lifetime apart. She could see it all: the tremor in Eleanor's hands, the glisten in Henry's eyes, the quiet miracle of reunion.

When the final chord faded, the applause was warm, sincere. Clara looked up, meeting Annabell's gaze in the audience, and smiled a silent thank-you.

Elias leaned close, whispering, "You, see? The music found its next voice."

Annabell nodded, her throat tight. "It always does."

Then it was time for The Symphony for Eleanor.

Annabell took her seat at the piano, Elias at the conductor's podium. The orchestra shimmered beneath the lights, poised and waiting. The moment was still, fragile, full of breath.

As she placed her fingers on the keys, she felt the faint tremble of anticipation does not fear, but reverence. The same piano stood before her, restored and polished, its surface reflecting the chandelier's soft glow. She took a deep breath and began.

The symphony unfolded differently this time slower, more contemplative, infused with the weight of years. Each movement carried a new resonance, shaped by the passage of time.

The opening Awakening still felt like morning, but now it was a gentler dawn, one that knew the beauty of the day because it had seen the night.

Memory and Light shimmered like autumn sunlight over water wistful, warm, alive with gratitude rather than grief.

When the orchestra reached Legacy, Elias's baton traced the air with precision and emotion. The brass swelled, the strings soared, and Annabell's piano answered not with the urgency of youth, but with the grace of understanding.

She felt the connection between them as tangibly as a pulse. Every look, every gesture between them carried the quiet intimacy of two souls who had built a lifetime together through music and trust.

As The Passage began, she felt tears prick her eyes. The motif from Eleanor's Waltz appeared again softly, almost hidden, a thread of continuity between all that had come before.

But then came something new a melody she had added recently, without telling Elias. A theme written for him. For their life together. For every late night and shared silence, every moment when love had been the truest sound in the room.

He looked at her when he heard it, his eyes widening slightly, then softening. His baton stilled for a beat just long enough for her to see his smile.

When the final note faded, the silence felt infinite.

And then the audience rose. Applause thundered, rolling through the hall like ocean waves.

But Annabell barely heard it. She turned to Elias, her eyes brimming. "That was for you," she whispered.

He reached out, touching her cheek lightly. "It always was," he said.

The crowd dispersed, they lingered in the empty ballroom. The chandeliers glowed dimmer now, their light softer, almost candle-like. The air carried the faint echo of applause, the lingering perfume of lilies.

Annabell sat on the edge of the stage, her heels clicking lightly against the marble. Elias joined her, setting his baton aside.

"Do you realize," she murmured, "that it's been forty years since I first walked into this hotel?"

He smiled. "Forty years since you heard a song and followed it."

She looked toward the piano. "Sometimes I think it was never really about the music. It was about finding the courage to listen to love without fear."

Elias's hand found hers. "And you did."

For a long moment, they sat in silence, surrounded by the hum of memory. Through the tall windows, the city glittered vast and alive, endlessly renewing itself.

Annabell thought of Eleanor and Henry of their young faces, their stolen dances, their decades apart, their reunion under these very lights. She thought of how love, when true, doesn't vanish. It becomes the air between notes, the heartbeat behind melody.

A soft smile touched her lips. "You know," she whispered, "I think they're dancing again tonight."

Elias looked toward the empty floor, and for just an instant, the chandeliers flickered. Two faint shapes moved together beneath the light graceful, ethereal, ageless.

Annabell felt warmth flood her chest. "They never left," she said softly.

He kissed her temple. "Neither will we."

They left the ballroom, the lights dimmed slowly behind them. The piano gleamed under the final glow, the program resting open on its lid:

100 Years of Eleanor's Waltz — The Legacy of Love and Time.

Outside, the city whispered beneath a silver moon. Annabell paused on the steps, breathing in the night. The air was cool, alive with the faint hum of traffic and possibility.

Elias slipped his arm around her shoulders. "Where to now?"

She smiled, eyes shining. "Wherever the next melody takes us."

They walked away hand in hand, their footsteps echoing faintly behind them not as an ending, but as a continuation.

And in the quiet that followed, the Waldorf seemed to sigh, its walls alive with the faint strains of music a waltz, soft and eternal, looping endlessly through time.

Love never ends. It simply finds a new refrain.

Epilogue — The Last Note

The house stood on a hill just outside Florence, the kind of place where time moved differently slower, gentler, as if the world had chosen to hum quietly rather than rush. Beyond the windows, olive trees swayed in the soft gold of the late afternoon. The air smelled of rosemary and sun-warmed stone.

Inside, Annabell Thorpe sat at a weathered piano, the same one she had bought years ago when she and Elias had finally decided to stop traveling. Its ivory keys had yellowed, its wood worn smooth by decades of music. A cup of tea cooled beside her, the steam curling lazily upward in the fading light.

On the stand before her rested a manuscript. The title, written in her graceful hand, read:

A Life in Time — The Memoirs of Annabell Thorpe

But that wasn't what she was working on at that moment. The manuscript was closed. Instead, she was writing music a final piece. Something that felt like a whisper, not a declaration.

Her fingers moved slowly, tentatively, tracing the edges of melody as if sketching a memory. The theme was quiet, circular a waltz that drifted without hurry, like leaves turning in the wind. She smiled faintly. It was both an ending and a beginning.

Elias's violin rested in its case near the window. He was gone now three years past, but she could still feel him in the air. In the way sunlight poured through the curtains. In the faint scent of varnish that never quite left the room.

Sometimes, when the wind came from the south, she swore she heard him humming. Other times, she thought she caught a bar or two of the Symphony for Eleanor echoing from somewhere beyond her hearing. It never frightened her. It comforted her.

Annabell paused, hands resting on the keys. The hill outside was bathed in the amber glow of twilight. She thought of everything that had led her here of New

York's glittering skyline, of the Waldorf ballroom, of the first trembling notes of Eleanor's Waltz that had changed everything.

She thought of Eleanor her Nana and of Henry, whose music had once carried their love across time. She thought of Elias, who had taught her that legacy wasn't a shadow to live under but a light to walk beside.

Her eyes misted, but her heart was full.

This, she realized, is what it means to have lived in music to have given love shape in sound, and to have left something beautiful behind.

When night came, she lit a single candle and continued to write. The new piece her last she called "The Last Note."

It was short. A gentle waltz that began with the theme from Eleanor's Waltz, then opened into something new her own motif, tender and luminous, bridging past and present. It was meant to be played quietly, almost as if it were being remembered rather than performed.

She imagined it being played long after she was gone perhaps by some young musician who found her music tucked away in an archive, unaware of its story. She hoped they would feel it the thread that connected generations, the pulse of love carried through time.

As she wrote the final bar, a soft breeze brushed through the open window. The candle flickered, and she looked up.

For a moment, she thought she saw them faint and radiant in the golden dusk.

Eleanor and Henry, swaying together in a slow, perfect dance. And behind them, Elias, smiling, violin in hand.

Tears spilled down her cheeks, but she was smiling too. "I was never alone," she whispered.

The figures seemed to shimmer brighter for a heartbeat then faded gently, like the last chord of a song.

Annabell placed her hand over the final note she had written and whispered, "Thank you."

Later, when the candle burned low, she closed her manuscript, set the new sheet atop it, and stood to gaze out the window. The moon hung high, silver and whole. The city lights far below glittered like distant music.

She thought of the words Elias once told her:

Music is the memory the world refuses to forget.

She smiled. "Then we'll never be forgotten."

The night was still. Somewhere, in the quiet, a piano note seemed to linger soft, steady, eternal.

Annabell sat once more and played The Last Note. Her fingers, though slower, still carried the same grace they always had. The melody flowed, warm and tender, filling the room with light.

As she reached the final chord, she let it hang not a farewell, but a breath. A pause that promised continuation.

In that silence, she finally felt it complete peace.

The next morning, the maid found her there, the sunrise spilling over her shoulders, her hand resting gently on the piano keys, her expression serene.

On the stand lay the finished score "The Last Note" and beside it, a letter addressed simply:

For those who come after —

Keep playing.

Love never ends.

— A.T.

Years later, when The Last Note was performed at the Waldorf Astoria the same hall where it had all begun critics wrote that it felt like sunlight distilled into sound. But those who knew the story understood.

They knew it wasn't an ending.

It was the final movement of an endless song a song begun by Eleanor and Henry,

carried by Annabell and Elias, destined to play on, quietly, in every heart that still believed in love.

As the last note faded, the chandeliers shimmered once more as if the music itself were smiling.

Because love, like music, never dies.

It simply finds new hands to play it.

Finis — but never the end.